Re

"Remember the night you said we made Caroline?" Eddie asked Grace timidly. "Remember you said you knew? That night? That you could feel that? I felt it too. I wanted to tell you that."

"Okay," Grace said, feeling his breath on her face.

"And remember when I asked you to marry me? I didn't think you'd say yes."

Her heart hurt her every time she thought about that. "But I did," she reminded him in a quiet murmur.

"I know. Don't you wonder if we could ever get back to that?"

Grace searched his eyes in the darkness, remembering how it had once been.

"Do you remember this?" Eddie took her face in his hands and kissed her. Her heart pounded as she moaned with passion.

"I do remember everything Eddie," she said, pressing him against the wall. "Everything . . ."

Something to Talk About

~

Deborah Chiel

Based on the screenplay
by Callie Khouri

A SIGNET BOOK

SIGNET
Published by the Penguin Group
Penguin Books USA Inc., 375 Hudson Street,
New York, New York 10014, U.S.A.
Penguin Books Ltd, 27 Wrights Lane,
London W8 5TZ, England
Penguin Books Australia Ltd, Ringwood,
Victoria, Australia
Penguin Books Canada Ltd, 10 Alcorn Avenue,
Toronto, Ontario, Canada M4V 3B2
Penguin Books (N.Z.) Ltd, 182-190 Wairau Road,
Auckland 10, New Zealand

Penguin Books Ltd, Registered Offices:
Harmondsworth, Middlesex, England

First published by Signet, an imprint of Dutton Signet,
a division of Penguin Books USA Inc.

First Printing, July, 1995
10 9 8 7 6 5 4 3 2 1

PUBLISHER'S NOTE
This is a work of fiction. Names, characters, places, and incidents either are the
product of the author's imagination or are used fictitiously, and any resemblance to
actual persons, living or dead, events, or locales is entirely coincidental.

BOOKS ARE AVAILABLE AT QUANTITY DISCOUNTS WHEN USED TO
PROMOTE PRODUCTS OR SERVICES. FOR INFORMATION PLEASE
WRITE TO PREMIUM MARKETING DIVISION, PENGUIN BOOKS USA
INC., 375 HUDSON STREET, NEW YORK, NY 10014.

If you purchased this book without a cover you should be aware that this book is
stolen property. It was reported as "unsold and destroyed" to the publisher
and neither the author nor the publisher has received any payment for this
"stripped book."

1
~

Some mornings, Grace King Bichon woke up with the image of herself at eighteen, galloping along the beach at Hilton Head. Except for a few determined runners and an occasional early-rising dog walker, the endless stretch of beach had belonged to her alone for that hour or two before she had to rejoin her family at the hotel where they were staying. She could still remember how free and unencumbered she'd felt then, with the sun rising over the Atlantic Ocean, a strong breeze blowing in her face, and her future spread out ahead of her. No dream had seemed too impractical, no obstacle too difficult to surmount. The possibilities had been as vast and limitless as the water lapping at the damp, pink sand beneath her horse's hooves.

She spent most of her waking hours around horses, but she couldn't recall when she'd last gone off to ride by herself, purely for pleasure. She hadn't been to the beach in years. She had hardly enough time to think about what the next hour might bring, let alone dwell on long-ago, unfulfilled adolescent dreams.

Especially now, with the Grand Prix only days away, she often had to stop and ask herself what she was supposed to do next. Today was no exception. She stared into the mirror, barely noticing the image reflected there of a twenty-eight-year-old woman with the huge brown eyes, full-lipped, generous mouth, and an unruly pile of long, dark hair she was plaiting into a tidy French braid. Blind to her own beauty, she peered critically at the faded white T-shirt, riding pants, and boots accessorized by the short strand of heirloom pearls.

The pearls were a last-minute concession to the Charity League meeting she had to attend later that morning. Everyone else would be dressed like the properly raised Southern women that they all were, herself included. But as the stable manager for one of the county's largest breeding farms, she could hardly show up for work in a dainty flowered skirt and high heels.

On most other women, her outfit would have looked ridiculous. But Grace King Bichon wasn't most other women. She moved with the ease and confidence of a competitive athlete. Her jodhpurs fit her like a second skin, and she still looked young enough to be chosen as the reigning queen of the season's debutante ball. She, of course, saw only the tiny crow's feet just beginning to form under her eyes, the stain on her shirt that no amount of bleach could remove, the scuffed boots that were in need of a good polish.

She absentmindedly fingered the pearls, a wedding gift from her mother, and tried to remember what it was she wanted to bring up at the meeting. Something about the cookbook. . . .

"So, what do you have on the docket for today?" Her husband's face loomed behind her in the mirror.

"Shit!" she yelled, startled by his sudden appearance. "Goddamn, Eddie! Will you make some noise or something?"

He scowled at her as he stepped forward to fix his tie. "Grace! Cut that out! Jesus Christ, you're gonna give me a heart attack!"

She glanced at him sideways, appreciating, in the abstract way of people who have been married long enough that they don't really notice each other, how handsome he looked. Almost thirty-five, he still exuded the boyish enthusiasm and irrepressible energy that had caught her eye the first time a sorority sister had pointed him out at a Greek Row dance. Eddie Bichon was one of the most sought-after men on campus. He wasn't at all her type, but he had flashed his devilish grin at her, asked her to dance, and she had been instantly smitten.

"I've got to go out to the barn," she said. "Daddy

wants to have some kind of a meeting with me and Hank about the Grand Prix."

"What about?" he said, fiddling with his tie.

She knew he was only asking to be polite. She could tell him her father wanted her to ride naked in the Grand Prix opening ceremonies, and he probably wouldn't even blink.

She twisted a rubber band around the end of her braid and said, "He just likes to start grinding us every year about this time. Makes him feel in control."

Eddie nodded, but his thoughts had clearly moved on to other matters. Except on those occasions when they entertained his clients, or he made the obligatory appearance at the twice-yearly horse show events, their work lives rarely intersected. It was just as well. Their very separate interests was probably what kept their marriage from getting stale.

Stepping away from the mirror, he asked, "Where's Doodlebug?"

Grace glanced at the clock radio next to their bed. Late again. "She better be getting dressed," she muttered. Today, especially, with all the forms she had sitting on her desk, she'd wanted to get an early start. "Caroline, what are you doing?" she shouted into the hallway.

As if on cue, their daughter bounded through the door, buttoning up her shirt. "Getting ready!" she sang out. "Am I going to ride?"

Grace planted a quick kiss on Caroline's head as she skipped past her. "If we have time."

Caroline was a miniature version of Grace—the same big eyes, full mouth, and stubborn will—and she lived to ride. But she had inherited her father's high spirits, and she was unabashedly Daddy's girl.

"Hey, Doodlebug!" said Eddie. He and Caroline had their special, private routines. "Where've you been all night?"

"Sleeping!" She giggled as she leaped into his welcoming embrace.

"What'd you dream about?" he asked, twirling her around the room.

"What do you think?" she shot back.

Grace gave herself the luxury of a moment to gaze indulgently at her daughter and husband, the two most important compass points in her universe. Their mutual adoration society was a club from which she was pointedly excluded, a state of affairs that only occasionally irritated her. Her relationship with her own father was complicated, and she had always been closer to her mother. Watching Caroline laughing in Eddie's arms, she felt a pang of envy for what she had never had with Wyly.

Eddie gave his daughter a warm hug and one last kiss, then lowered her back to the floor.

"Hey," Grace said as Caroline raced out of the room, her legs flashing behind her like a frisky pony. "I have to take her to Miller's today to get fitted for her riding suit. You want to meet us there, and then we can take her to lunch?"

Eddie shook his head regretfully. "I can't do lunch. I've got a meeting I can't get out of. Do you want to meet before?"

"Can't. Got a Charity League meeting. They stuck me with chairman of the Cookbook Committee."

"How 'bout tomorrow?" Eddie suggested.

"Tomorrow's Saturday," she reminded him.

"Got a golf game."

As if she didn't know that. Eddie had played golf with the same three frat buddies from college every Saturday morning for almost as long as they'd been married.

"How's Monday?" he asked.

Grace shrugged. "If I can stave her off that long." Monday was fine, but today would have been better. She doubted Eddie would understand why, even if she tried to explain it to him.

Buying Caroline's riding suit at Miller's was a rite of passage, a special occasion that she'd wanted all three of them to celebrate together. This year's Grand Prix would be her first competition on the national level, a big step forward for a young rider, even one as accomplished as Caroline. Grace wanted her to savor all the surrounding hoopla, along with every moment of the event itself.

"Okay," Eddie said, too involved in looking for his briefcase to see the disappointment on her face.

"Call June and have her schedule it. Are you going to cook tonight?"

She hadn't thought that far ahead. Dinner was hours away, and she had to much to do before then. "Depends. Are you going to be here?"

"I'll call you," he said, checking his watch.

"Okay."

Time to go, or they'd both be late. More and more lately, their lives seemed to be ruled by the clock. How had they gotten so busy that she had to call her husband's secretary in order to make a lunch date with him? Maybe she should have June pencil in an appointment for them to make love.

She sighed as she stepped out onto the porch. The weather was unseasonably warm for this late in the fall, even for South Carolina. A mild wind blowing in from the west rustled the branches of the Spanish moss-draped oaks that surrounded their Georgian-style mansion, which she'd painstakingly restored in midnineteenth century antebellum style.

Eddie's parents had bought them the house in honor of Caroline's birth and generously offered to pay for the services of Mrs. Bichon's own interior designer. But Grace had insisted on doing the work herself. She had studied domestic photographs and paintings of the period, lingered over every paint sample and fabric swatch, and studied the contractor's blueprints as if they'd held the key to her happiness. Her efforts had been judged so authentic that the ladies of the Historical Society had begged to have the house included in their annual Fall Tour of Homes and Plantations.

Flattered to have been asked, Grace nevertheless firmly declined. She shuddered at the prospect of strangers walking through her rooms, ogling her furniture and wallpaper, poking into the corners of her family's life as if they were three-dimensional figures in a museum diorama.

Decorating the house had been a labor of love. She had been slightly embarrassed to discover it was being touted as a showpiece, or so it had been described by the local gossips. All she had meant to do was create a comfortable home for her family, a place for people to gather and laugh and enjoy themselves. A home like the one in which she had grown up.

She looked across the yard at the woods that bordered the far end of their property. The sun had just risen above the trees, which were only now beginning to lose their riotous autumn color. She watched as a squirrel scurried across the lawn and vanished into the woods. It was a glorious day to be outside, a gift from the gods that came too seldom. She had the crazy impulse to grab Eddie by the arm and disappear with him into the woods, to play hooky from all their responsibilities.

Instead, she kissed him good-bye and followed him down the steps of the porch to their respective cars. He got into his Mercedes. She got into her

Jeep. With the precision of a carefully choreographed routine, they simultaneously began driving out of the driveway. Halfway to the road, Grace realized with a start that something was missing from the picture. Mentally berating herself, she slammed on the brakes, reversed, and backed up to the house.

Where was her brain today? She hurried onto the porch and unlocked the front door. Her guilt increased by geometric proportions as she was confronted by Caroline, crouched on the floor in the foyer. She glared up at Grace, her little face a study in hurt indignation.

Lord in heaven! What kind of a terrible mother must she be to leave the house and forget all about her daughter?

~

It was easier for Caroline to forgive Grace than it was for Grace to forgive herself. While Caroline chattered on about her new riding habit, she continued to brood over her absentmindedness as they pulled onto the road that led to her parents' home, just a short distance away from their own. The sign on the entrance gate provided Grace with a minor but ongoing source of irritation. Under the silhouetted drawing of a sleek-limbed thoroughbred horse were the words KING FARMS. Beneath that, in slightly smaller letters, the inscription declared, WYLY KING—OWNER. A third line, in even smaller lettering, read, HANK CORRIGAN—TRAINER.

Grace kept waiting for a fourth line to be added: GRACE KING BICHON—STABLE MANAGER. Too proud to ask and run the risk that her father might turn her down, she knew that hell would freeze over before he would think of it himself. The omission was typical of Wyly—and of the peculiar dynamic that marked their relationship. He relied heavily on her administrative expertise, trusted her judgment, but kept the reins of power as firmly in his grasp as if he were breaking a wild stallion.

She knew he'd be lost without her. King Farms was a family affair: her mother kept the books, while her younger sister, Emma Rae, ran the estate auction and real estate end of the business. But Grace had an intuitive understanding of horses that surpassed even Wyly's considerable knowledge. She wondered, not for the first time, whether Wyly would have been quicker to add a son's name to the sign on the gate. Then she reminded herself, also not for the first time, that change came slowly, especially in the South.

The long, sweeping driveway, which was lined with oak and pecan trees, led to the barn where the horses were stabled, and beyond that to her childhood home. Grace had barely pulled to a stop before Caroline was out of the jeep and dashing for the barn. Grace let her go. She remembered how it felt to be eight years old and so madly in love with a horse named Boots that she'd carried a picture of him in her wallet and couldn't go to sleep before she'd kissed him good night.

Before they headed into town, they would drop by the house to say hello to her mother. Now, the hubbub and commotion of the stable area immediately claimed her attention. A half-dozen men were already hard at work there. A couple of them she had known all her life, the others for half that time or more. Blunt and quick-tempered, Wyly King wasn't the easiest person in the world to get along with. But he was generally acknowledged to be honest and fair, and he treated his employees as well as he treated the prize-winning horses he bred and trained. Once hired, the men didn't leave unless they had a damn good reason to quit.

"Hey, Dub," she called.

Dub, a short, ruddy-faced man who used to swing her onto his shoulders and take her to visit the horses, smiled a greeting. "Morning, Grace."

"Harry," she said to one of the grooms. "Take the trailer over to the Macks' to pick up Joe's Whimsey around four-thirty. Sheila'll ride over here with you and help him get squared away."

Harry looked up from the bridle he was cleaning. "Yes, ma'am."

"Tell Hank before you go, so he can be here," she told him.

He nodded. "No problem."

She waved at the other men and stopped for a minute to pat the horses that had been led outside to be groomed. Then she went into the barn to face the mountains of papers waiting for her on her desk.

~

Caroline was perched outside a stall on a mounting step that gave her the height she needed to commune at eye level with her favorite horse. The plaque on the door said the stall belonged to Silver Bells. But the horse's silvery gray color and pink nose had earned him the more commonly used nickname of Possum, which Caroline was cooing in his ear as she stroked his face.

A beautiful animal, with a long curved neck and a wide chest, he was a Trakehner, the offspring of two prize-winning jumpers and had already begun to fulfill the promise of his championship heritage. But Caroline's feelings about him had nothing to do with bloodlines. For her, it had been love at first sight, a chemical reaction between a one-year-old girl and a weak-kneed foal sprawled in the straw, too newly born into the world to stand on its own legs.

Other children her age had stuffed animals, imaginary best friends, or siblings with whom they shared their deepest fears and confidences. Caroline poured out the secrets of her heart into Possum's ears and dreamed of the day she would ride him in competition. When that day might come was currently a matter of some conflict between Caroline and her mother.

"Possum," she whispered, plying him with carrots as she imagined herself proudly mounted on his back.

He was nuzzling her pockets for the goodies he was used to finding there when the big door at the far end of the barn slid open. Wyly King strode down the breezeway toward his granddaughter.

"Caught ya!" he declared, his blue eyes crinkling in the smile he always had for her. "You trying' to bribe ol' Possum?"

"Hey, Gramps," she said happily.

He watched her feed Possum another handful of carrots and shook his head. "Miss Lily's gonna get jealous and dump you off in the ring," he warned. "You gotta save the treats for the horse you're gonna ride."

Standing on the mounting step, she was almost his height. Now, she suddenly turned to face him and grabbed him by his vest.

"Gramps! Why? Please let me!" she pleaded, determined to win him over as her ally. "I don't want to ride a pony! I want to ride a horse! There's kids younger than me already."

He stared at her, finding in her features a duplication of his older daughter. She was every bit as obstinate as Grace, as well. He normally gave her whatever she asked for, often slipping her forbidden treats behind her parents' backs. But it was up to Grace to decide which horse Caroline rode in competition, and for once, he and Grace were in total agreement.

"Now, honey, hold on a minute. First of all, you can *win* on Miss Lilly." He picked her up from the step, and she wrapped her legs about his waist, an old trick of theirs. But when had she gotten so heavy? "Oh, good Lord," he groaned, straining to carry her. "Let me put you down."

Caroline responded by squeezing her legs even more tightly around him. He winced, but she refused to loosen the viselike grip she had on him. "See? See how strong my legs are?" she said.

He was actually beginning to feel some pain. Now it was his turn to plead. "Honey, I gotta put you down! Have mercy on an old man."

Her point made, she let go and dropped to the floor. Wyly took a deep breath, rubbed his waist, and regained his composure. "And second, he's too damn big for you," he said, warming up to one of his favorite themes. "You've gotta learn to recognize your limitations—"

"How old was Mama when she won on Sunny Girl?" Caroline interrupted him.

"Nine." He smiled. He'd been so proud of Grace on that bright September day, the beginning of such a long string of wins that he'd lost track of them. But the first one he would never forget.

"How much did she weigh?" Caroline asked skeptically.

"Honey, I don't remember." The child was relentless! She was too young to understand the difference between taking a risk and meeting a challenge. Miss Lilly was the right size for a little thing like Caroline. There would be plenty of time for her to ride the bigger horses.

"Now don't get yourself all worked up! You're gonna have to take this up with your mama. Have you done that?"

"Yes." She pouted.

"And?"

She stuck her hands on her hips and glared at him. "You think I'd be down here beggin' you if she'd said yes? Just put me on that horse, and I'll win Youth Classic championship! And how come everybody thinks they gotta tell me when I'm ready?" she demanded, her voice rising with indignation. "I tell *you* when I'm ready! And I'm ready! And I'm about runnin' out of patience with you people!"

Dub had sauntered into the barn in time to hear the end of her tantrum. He exchanged a look of amusement with Wyly as Caroline suddenly realized she'd crossed way over the line of good manners. She was a kid, and kids were definitely not allowed to raise their voices to their elders. She cut herself short and set her lips, waiting for her grandfather's reprimand.

But Wyly grinned good-humoredly. He had mellowed over the years and was far more lenient with his only grandchild than he had been with his daughters. "Who's that remind you of?" he asked Dub.

Dub rubbed his chin. "It's uncanny."

"Go give Dub a hand and earn your keep around here," Wyly said. "I gotta talk to your mama now."

Relieved to have gotten off without a scolding, Caroline turned away.

"Hey!" Wyly shouted. "Come back here and kiss your grandpa. I oughta swat you one for carryin' on this way."

He raised his hand. Caroline knew he'd never make good on his threat and didn't even flinch as Wyly swept her up into his arms for a kiss.

The child was the best gift his daughter had ever given him. Being a grandfather was all fun and no responsibility. He grinned again as she slipped Possum another carrot and peeked at him under her arm, thinking she'd put one over on him. At the rate she was feeding the damn horse, he'd soon be too fat to compete. But there was no stopping Caroline. She was just like her mother. She was a winner, all right. It was in her blood.

His head trainer came riding into the barn, which reminded Wyly of his next order of business. "Hey, Hank!" he greeted him. "How's it goin'?"

Hank Corrigan hopped off his horse and handed

the reins to Dub, who led the horse away to the grooming area, with Caroline trailing behind him. Hank squinted warily at his boss. "Good," he said. "Great."

A trimly built man in his early forties whose face was a map of crisscrossing lines, the natural effect of a life spent working outdoors, he was one of the best trainers money could hire. But Wyly had a nasty habit of second-guessing him, and the two men were often at odds with each other. He knew from experience that when Wyly went out of his way to be friendly, he was generally up to something that Hank wasn't going to like.

"Good!" Wyly boomed. "Grace needs to see you."

"Now?"

"In a bit. I've gotta talk to her for a minute. After that."

"Yes, sir," said Hank.

Wyly could feel Hank staring after him as he walked across the barn to his daughter's office. He had made his decision, and he had no qualms about it. He had waited too long for this shot not to grab hold of it. Sure, Hank might be upset—even angry. But at his age, he had earned the right to stop worrying about whether someone's nose was out of joint. And hell, it was his damn farm, wasn't it?

With that thought in mind, he marched into

Grace's office and planted himself in front of her desk.

Grace looked up from the pile of Grand Prix entry forms that needed her signature and wondered what mischief her father was up to this morning.

At sixty-five, he was still one of the most handsome men she had ever seen, with flowing white hair, features that were chiseled and aged to perfection, and a vigor that much younger men would envy. "Aged to perfection," he liked to say about himself.

She loved him dearly and respected his years of accumulated wisdom about horse breeding. But he often acted on impulse, then left it to her or Emma Rae to deal with the consequences of his sudden brainstorms. The steely glint in his blue eyes was all the warning she needed that he was about to dump another cleanup operation in her lap.

"Hi, Daddy," she said.

Wyly shut the door to her office.

She thought, uh-oh, this was *really* serious, and steeled herself for the inevitable bad news.

There was no "good morning," no chitchat about Caroline or the weather. Wyly got right down to business. "All right. Have a Heart went on the market last week."

"Yeah?"

"The one from California, Jamie Johnson's

22

horse. He won the Hampton Classic in September."

"I know the horse. How much is he askin'?"

"One hundred and fifty thousand."

At that price, the horse was a steal. She would have guessed two hundred thousand, at least. "That's all? What's wrong with him?"

Wyly shook his head. "Nothing. Johnson's having to sell 'cause of his divorce. Anyway . . ." He grinned, a little boy caught with his hand in the cookie jar. "I bought him."

"You did *what?*" He had to be kidding . . . except that Wyly never joked about buying horses.

He crossed his arms against his chest as if to fend off her anger. "I've just got a feeling about him. I think this is his year. He's got Grand Prix Champion written all over him. And . . ."

His momentary pause was long enough for her to guess the worst was still to come.

"I'm gonna' ride him," he said defiantly.

His announcement propelled her out of her chair. "But, Daddy, without even discussing it with us?"

"There's nothing to discuss." He knew he'd dropped a bombshell. He had had a lot of experience with this sort of thing. He fell silent, giving Grace a chance to absorb the information.

How many times while she was growing up had she heard that very same line? *There's nothing to discuss.* How often had Wyly appointed himself the one and only arbiter, the judge *and* jury in a system where the case was closed before she ever had a chance to argue her side?

Tears streaming down her cheeks, filled with despair, she would go running to her mother for comfort. Her mother's response was always the same: she would dry Grace's tears with her lightly scented handkerchief, give her a hug, and remind her that Daddy only needed to *think* he was getting his way—because he was so sure his was the right way. Men had funny ideas about being in charge, Georgia King would say, pouring Grace a glass of iced tea. No point in fighting that notion, when she could win the battle by other, much more subtle means.

And it was true that though Wyly thundered his pronouncements like an Old Testament prophet delivering the word of the Lord to the Israelites, she and Emma Rae usually wound up doing or buying whatever it was he'd originally told them they couldn't.

This felt different, though. This problem wasn't simply between herself and Wyly. Too much was at stake: money, ego, the reputation of King Farms, a long-standing relationship with a valuable employee who couldn't be easily replaced. It would take more sweet-talking than she had in her repertoire to placate Hank Corrigan once he got wind of Wyly's scheme.

"Jesus H. Christ, Daddy! What are you talking about? What about Ransom? Hank's going to—"

The door suddenly flew open. Caroline bounded into the office. "Mom? Dub said I could—"

"Not now, honey!" Grace said, firmly pushing her out and closing the door in her face.

"Ransom's not ready," Wyly said as smoothly as if they had not been interrupted. "I don't have the same feeling about him."

It hadn't even occurred to him to consult her or Hank! "What have the last five years been about? He's had a great year," she reminded him.

Wyly glowered at her challenge to his authority. "That's enough!" he snapped. "Now, I've been doin' this since you were tapping on a high chair with a teaspoon! I'm doin' what I'm doin'!"

A kaleidescope of furious responses whirled through Grace's mind. She was tempted to tell him what she was thinking: that he was being high-handed, selfish, shortsighted. She wanted to throw the pile of forms at him, stomp out of the office, and leave him to take care of his own damn mess. Instead, she tried to reason with him.

"Daddy, Hank doesn't have time to take on another horse this close to the show."

"He doesn't have to," said Wyly, calmer now that he'd laid down the law for Grace. "Jamie Johnson is bringing him himself. He's gonna work with him until after the show. That was part of the deal. He's coming tomorrow with the horse

25

and the rest of his barn is coming out later. Fourteen altogether. Have Dub hire as many extra grooms as it's gonna take."

"You're going to ride against Hank and Ransom?" she asked disbelievingly.

"No." He frowned, annoyed that Grace was being so pigheaded that she refused to believe he meant business. "We're not gonna enter Ransom. Not this year. He can wait another year."

Grace gripped the edge of the desk to steady herself. In the five years she'd been stable manager, Wyly had made some pretty dumb judgment calls. For plain asinine stupidity, this one ranked high above the rest of them. If she didn't know better, she would think he was getting senile.

"That doesn't make any sense! Let's enter them both," she urged him.

"Honey, when this is your place, you can do whatever you want."

Another line she'd heard from him too often to count. He would have been shocked and insulted if she told him the truth. She could walk the land in the dark on a moonless night and never got lost. The mingled aromas of magnolia and hay and horses were as familiar to her as the natural fragrance of her daughter's skin. But she never wanted to own the farm.

She had agreed to be the stable manager only because it seemed foolish to hire some stranger who couldn't do the job half as well as she could.

But one of these days, before she got too old and lost her nerve, she had to find something that was totally her own, that hadn't come to her because she was Wyly King's daughter, or Mrs. Eddie Bichon. Work here for the rest of her life? Thanks, but no thanks.

"Daddy," she said softly. "Hank will quit."

"Well, honey, here's a good opportunity for you to utilize your people skills. You see to it that he doesn't. You hear me? You understand?"

She refused to be seduced by his flattery. "You can't do this. It's not fair!"

"It's done," he said. "Now roll with it." He opened the door and left the office before she could say another word.

She imagined herself walking away from her job. It would serve him right if both she and Hank quit. The fantasy was momentarily tempting. But she couldn't do that to her father, who had given her so many wonderful opportunities and so much encouragement.

She slammed her hand on the top of the desk. "Goddamn son-of-a-fucking-bitch! Shit! Shit! Shit!" she muttered.

The door flew open, and Wyly leaned into the room. "You watch that mouth now," he said.

He was whistling as he passed the grooming area on his way out of the barn. "Hey, Hank," he cheerfully hailed the trainer. "She can see you now."

The next few minutes were even more unpleasant than Grace had anticipated. She had barely stumbled through an explanation of what she didn't understand herself when Hank exploded with a string of profanities longer and louder than her own.

"Well, then, goddamnit, I quit! I don't need this shit!" he shouted as he charged out of her office and through the breezeway.

"Hank, wait!" Grace yelled. Already late for her Charity League meeting, she raced after him, hoping to effect even a temporary truce.

"I wish the son of a bitch would die in a fiery car crash!" he growled as she caught up with him.

"I know, Hank," she agreed, not even trying to hide her resentment. "Get in line. But just listen—"

"No!" He shoved his finger under her nose. "You listen! I'm not gonna just sit by while this son of a bitch ruins my career! This is Ransom's year! This is it! I know like I know my own—"

"He may change his mind again when the horse gets here," she broke in. "You know how he is!"

He punched the air with his fist as he spat out the words. "What I know is that I've been busting my ass from sunup to sundown for the last fifteen years for the son of a bitch, and now he pulls a chicken shit maneuver like this! Well, he can kiss my ass!"

Desperate to defuse his rage, she begged, "Hank, please! Give me some time! Maybe I can make him see reason!"

"Like hell," he said bitterly.

She pictured herself single-handedly taking care of all the complicated arrangements for the upcoming Grand Prix and almost burst into tears. "You can't do this to me!" she wailed.

A car pulled up behind them. "Grace!" Her sister poked her head out the window and called, "Is Daddy in there?"

"No!" she said, and went right back to pressing her argument with the trainer. "Please, for God's sake, Hank. Give me some time! I'll do . . . something."

He glowered at her, then marched back to the barn, swearing under his breath. She didn't blame him; her promise rang as ineffectual in her ears as it must have in his. But she *would* make good on it. She wasn't about to lose Hank Corrigan, not even for as fine a horse as Have a Heart.

"Grace, hold on a sec!" shouted Emma Rae, who had pulled up right behind her.

"I can't!" Grace shook her head as she slid into her car and fished for her keys. "I have a Charity League meeting!" Suddenly, struck with an ugly suspicion, she angled around to face her sister. "Did you know about this, Emma Rae?" she asked.

"What? About this horse thing?"

Her anger and frustration hit boiling point. "Thanks a lot for telling me!" she lashed out at her sister.

But Emma Rae was not an easy target. "Hey! Check your machine, Grace!" she yelled.

Damn! The red light on her answering machine had been blinking when she'd left the house, but she had been in too much of a rush to listen to the message. It would have helped to have been prepared for Wyly's announcement. The surprise had worked to his advantage.

She leaned her head against the steering wheel and wondered why she couldn't keep all the different pieces of her life from bumping into each other. How did other women manage? She wished she could raise the subject at a Charity League meeting, but that was precisely the sort of question that never seemed to get talked about there. If other women were having trouble, they sure as hell weren't admitting it.

Smiling at the image of the League ladies reformatting themselves into a support group, she started the car and began backing out of the driveway.

"Grace! Wait!" Emma Rae called to her.

She decided no, and sped down the driveway. She didn't have the time or the patience right now to spend one more second discussing Wyly's crazy decision, and how she was going to make everything okay again.

When she reached the main road, she braked and checked the oncoming traffic before she turned right to head into town. A horn blared loudly enough to make her glance in her rear-view mirror. There was Emma Rae again, waving at her through the open window. Her passenger side front door flew open. Caroline leaped out of the car and came running over to catch up with Grace.

"Oh, God." That made twice in one morning she'd forgotten her daughter. She was a terrible mother. Poor Caroline! She was probably developing all kinds of complexes. The child could be traumatized for life!

She rubbed her forehead with her fingers. "Help me, Lord," she muttered and consoled herself with the thought that from here on in, this day could only get better.

2

~

The Charity League was headquartered in a quaint, elegantly furnished house in the heart of the city's historic district, where most of the homes dated back to the early nineteenth century. The organization had come into existence in 1893, when ten generous-spirited ladies from several of the city's best families had undertaken to provide aid to the needy and sick. In its earliest days, membership was restricted to those who could trace their roots in the county for at least two generations. Though the powers who ruled the League still shuddered at the notion of a Yankee joining their ranks, in more recent years the ladies had been forced to adjust their standards and extend fellowship to some relative newcomers.

Nevertheless, the League was still considered one of the area's most venerable and exclusive institutions. Caroline's grandmothers on both sides had belonged, and her mother and Great-aunt Rae continued to be actively involved. Some traditions were too important to discard. Even Emma Rae, who seemed to thrive on breaking the rules, had gotten herself appropriately decked out for the annual New Members garden party and had taken the oath that bound her to uphold the League's principles. Grace had received her own engraved invitation shortly after her twenty-first birthday. She had gladly accepted the honor, and dutifully appeared at the meetings even when they played havoc with her schedule.

The large wood-paneled room, formerly the library of the family that had deeded the house to the League, was filled to capacity with women ranging in age from twenty-one to eighty. For many of them, the League meetings were a focal point of their social life, an excuse to get out of the house, see friends, gossip, show off a new outfit. Grace counted herself lucky if she could grab a few minutes to catch up with Lucy Bales, her best friend since second grade, during the refreshments part of the meeting.

Today, as happened so often lately, she found her mind wandering during the speakers' reports and presentations. It was hard to concentrate on Barbaranelle Caldwell's plans for the spring flea market when all she could think about was how to resolve the fight between Wyly and Hank.

She hoped that Eddie would be home for dinner tonight so she could get his advice. She'd read an article in *Cosmo* a while back that had posed the question: "Did You Marry a Man Just Like Dear Old Dad?" Close enough, she'd decided after skimming the accompanying checklist. Eddie and Wyly were both charming, willful men who were used to getting their way, most especially with the women in their lives. Well, fine. If they were so much alike, Eddie could give her some insights about how to handle her father.

A voice gradually filtered through her awareness. She tuned back in time to hear the League president, Norma Leggett, declare, ". . . and a great big thanks for Jessie Gaines and her husband Happy for the absolutely beautiful job they did repainting the children's ward! The stenciling is absolutely wonderful!"

She joined in the applause for Jessie, who purred with pleasure at the recognition. Then Norma continued, "Now, to the business of the centennial cookbook. I know we all want this to be our best ever, so I'll ask our committee chairman to bring us up to date. Grace?"

Of course, she'd forgotten she was supposed to give a report today on the damn cookbook, which was the main reason she was seated at the front of the room, alongside the other committee chairmen. She stopped fidgeting with her pearls, stood up, and tried not to feel foolish about showing up in her riding pants when everyone else had so obviously dressed up for the meeting.

"Well," she said, stalling as she struggled to recall what she needed to tell them. She pictured a calendar and then she remembered. "The deadline for recipe submissions is December 2, and it would help if they were typed."

There was a collective groan from the audience. Few of the women knew how to type. But their last cookbook had been riddled with errors because the typist had misread so many of the recipes. After numerous complaints about brunches and dinner parties spoiled by dishes that were too salty, too sweet, or wouldn't rise when they were supposed to, the League had been forced to issue a public apology. The board wasn't about to make the same mistake.

"Also, if you want to substitute vegetable shortening wherever it says bacon grease or lard, you might want to think about that," Grace went on. "Nell McGeehee asked me to mention that, because her husband Bobby is recovering from a triple bypass right now. Also, Lucy is taking over for me until after the Grand Prix. I'm up to my neck in horses till then. I think that's it."

Lucy shook her head. "Names," she said.

Grace looked at her quizzically. "What?"

"Names!" Lucy reiterated.

"Oh, right. Well, the committee thinks . . ." She cast about for the best way to present what was bound to raise a lot of controversy. "We've looked at a lot of other cookbooks . . . and we've always been listed with our married names underneath the recipe. And frankly, the practice of excluding our first names . . . it looks outdated. We want to just list our names, first, middle, and last. That's all."

A few of the younger women clapped. Otherwise, her announcement was met with mostly uneasy glances, then a strained silence.

"Does this have something to do with Hillary?" asked Mary Jane Archer, whose husband was the Republican party state chairman.

"I always thought the way it was looked quaint." Edna Carter defended the practice.

The women erupted in a cacophonous discussion of conflicting opinions that reminded Grace of the squawkings of a flock of geese.

"It doesn't look quaint, Edna." Nadine Hester, a friend of Grace's mother, sprang to Grace's defense. "It looks antiquated! I don't see why Harry's name should be in a cookbook. He'd no more lift a finger to cook than to poke himself in the eye with a sharp stick."

"But what about the tradition?" whined Kitty Coleman, one of Grace's contemporaries, whose oldest daughter was named after Scarlet O'Hara.

"Why carry on a tradition if it's stupid and insulting? I've got a name, and I want it in the goddamn cookbook!" Lucy said loudly.

Barbaranelle, sporting too much jewelry and makeup as usual, pulled herself to her feet, her unsteady stance lending support to the rumor that she mixed her morning glass of orange juice with a heavy dose of vodka. "What I'd like to know," she demanded, "is if my name isn't in there—Mrs. Franklin J. Caldwell, III—how the hell is anybody gonna know who I am? I mean, Barbaranelle Caldwell . . . who's that? It could be his daughter, for heaven's sake."

"You wish," muttered Lorene Rhiner.

"Shut up, Lorene," Barbaranelle hissed, plopping herself back down in her chair.

"What about that thing of putting our first names in parentheses after our married names?" proposed Mary Jane.

Nadine hooted scornfully. "Like an afterthought. Yeah, that'll look real contemporary. Hey, did you hear they've invented an engine that runs on steam?"

Grace felt like putting her hands to her ears and screaming at them to be quiet. Raising the issue had been mostly Lucy's idea, but the more she listened to the arguments pro and con, the more strongly she felt about the outcome. Lucy and Nadine were absolutely right. "Mrs. Eddie Bichon" didn't begin to express who she was. She had her own name, her own identity, and she was damn proud of it.

She waved her hand to reclaim the floor. "Well, my name is going in there, Grace King Bichon," she announced. "I don't care what anybody else does!"

"Well, now," said Norma, who was well practiced in restoring peace among the members. "Let's all calm down. This isn't something that's going to be decided today. If there's no further business, then this meeting is adjourned." She lavished a wide smile on her ladies and clapped enthusiastically, as if in recognition of *all* their good efforts on behalf of the League.

The topic wasn't so easily shelved, however. The discussion continued as the women rose to leave.

"Hell, I'm proud to use my husband's name. I consider the fact that I'm still married to the old goat one of my greatest accomplishments," Barbaranelle declared.

Grace and Lucy glanced at each other. "What year is this?" murmured Grace.

"No shit," Lucy said.

Shaking their heads in dismay, they trailed the others out of the room. A small knot of women stood in the hallway, oohing and aahing over the diamond-and-sapphire-studded tennis bracelet that hung on Edna's wrist.

"Lord have mercy. Either you've been really good, or he's been really bad," teased Barbaranelle.

Lorene winked knowingly. "That is some major guilt there."

"He bought it from Calhoun. Want me to find out how much it cost?" offered Mary Jane.

Edna smirked as she extended her arm for all to see. "I tell you, the bigger a rascal he is, the better the birthday present."

"Well, if that's the way it works, that puts us in the running for the Hope Diamond," Lucy cracked with a wry smile as she and Grace walked away from the group.

"Speak for yourself," Grace said. Maybe Andy Bales had the time to run around on Lucy, but Eddie's dad kept him much too busy making real estate deals for him to have an affair.

The basement of the house, once a warren of cubicles where the slaves had slept, had been gutted and transformed into a playroom. Today, because of the teachers' conference that had kept Caroline out of school, the room was crowded with children and their mothers who'd come to claim them.

"Hey, Aunt Rae, I didn't see you when we came in! How are you?" Grace greeted her great-aunt, who bustled over with Caroline in tow.

Aunt Rae, her maternal grandmother's younger sister, was a spry, peppery-tongued seventy-five-year-old who went riding every day in almost every kind of weather, volunteered three times a week in the League gift shop, and kept the doctor busy with a never-ending litany of symptoms, each more fantastical than the next.

"Oh, fine as can be," she said now, managing to imply she was battling some new and undiagnosed illness. "You know, your mother called. She wants to change the menu for the Grand Prix party."

Grace suddenly realized she'd left the farm without visiting her mother. Georgia probably had wanted to talk to her about the party the Kings always hosted on the last night of the Grand Prix competition.

"What for? Everybody loves it," she said, chiding herself for her thoughtlessness.

Aunt Rae shrugged. "She wants shrimp. She said she's just sick to death of ham and barbecue. They've been doin' it that way for thirty-five years, I don't know why it suddenly bothers her now." Abruptly switching gears, she patted Caroline on the head and said, "Bring this little precious thing over to my house and let me give her some lunch."

"Mom," Caroline said nervously.

Grace squeezed Caroline's hand to reassure her. "I've got to take her down to Pinkerton's to get her fitted for her riding habit. I promised," she told Aunt Rae.

Aunt Rae beamed at Caroline. "Well, that's wonderful! Who're you gonna ride?"

"Possum," said Caroline at the exact same moment that Grace said, "Miss Lily."

Grace rolled her eyes. "No, you're not, young lady. We've been through this a thousand and one times!"

"Is this because I don't have all my teeth?" Caroline sulked.

"We're not going to discuss this," Grace said firmly.

Caroline's mouth contorted into a pout. "But why?"

"No!" She silenced Caroline with a stern gaze, then turned to Aunt Rae and said, "We better get going. I hate to fight with my child in public."

Aunt Rae gave Caroline a big hug. Then she bent down and whispered in her ear the same words of wisdom she'd shared with Grace when Grace was about her age. "You gotta wear them down."

~

The city's business district was concentrated around the edges of its nineteenth-century core. A grouping of modest skyscrapers overlooking the river stood like a glass-and-steel bulwark that kept the present from committing any further incursions on the past. Most of the buildings had sprung up during Grace's childhood, and whenever she drove downtown she felt a pang of nostalgia for the ramshackle old warehouses that once had held the cotton crops of the wealthy farmers and plantation owners.

"Keep your eyes peeled for a parking spot, sweetie plum," she told Caroline as they approached the block where Miller's Equestrian Shop had been located since before she was born.

"Yuck. That's gross, Mom," said Caroline, who had been daydreaming aloud all the way into town about becoming a prize-winning rider on the Grand Prix circuit.

Grace smiled. "I know, but Gram used to say it to me, and now it's a habit. She'd also say, 'I'll keep an eye out for you.'"

"Gross," said Caroline as they pulled to a stop at a red light. "Why do buildings have stories?" she asked.

"What do you mean?" Grace turned sideways to look at her daughter, who was delicately exploring her right nostril with her index finger. "Don't pick your nose, honey."

Caroline craned her neck to get a better view of the office buildings. "Why do they say it's twenty stories or fifty stories high?" she said.

"That's a good question. I'm not sure why that is. We're going to have to look that one up," Grace said, searching the left side of the street for an empty space.

Then she caught sight of Eddie, standing with his back to her, staring at himself in the mirrored facade of one of the skyscrapers. Before she had a chance to call out to him, a young woman in a red crepe suit emerged from the building, hurried over, and gave Eddie a little tug on the ear. He turned around and smiled at the young woman, then put his arms around her waist, pulled her closer to him, and gave her a long kiss on the lips.

Eddie whispered something in the woman's ear, and the woman slid her arm around his shoulder. Grace's mouth dropped open. As if she were watching a love scene in a movie, she waited for one of them to make the next move.

Suddenly, she realized that she had to prevent Caroline from seeing Eddie. Trying to keep her voice steady, she pointed to a sign on the other side of the street and said, "What's that sign say, ladybug? Can you read what that says?"

She sneaked a peek at Eddie and the woman, who looked very comfortable together, walking arm-in-arm.

"Un . . . Un . . . I . . . on. Onion. Onion Street," said Caroline, sounding out the word as Eddie stopped to kiss the woman again. The woman nodded, as if agreeing to something he'd said earlier, and they turned into the parking lot behind the building.

"No, honey. Union. That's Union Street," Grace quietly corrected her daughter.

Eddie and the woman had disappeared now, but she couldn't seem to tear her eyes away from the spot where she'd last seen them kissing. She couldn't breathe properly. She kept sucking in air, but there was nowhere for it to go. She felt as if the wind had been knocked out of her, the way she'd felt once when she'd fallen off a galloping horse and smashed her chest against a rock.

"Mom, green means go," Caroline said impatiently.

A horn honked behind her. Grace finally caught her breath. She stared at her hands, which were clenched around the steering wheel. For a second, she couldn't remember what she was supposed to do, and then she remembered. *Drive,* she told herself. She took her foot off the brake and jammed it onto the gas pedal. The car lurched forward through the intersection.

"Union," said Caroline, matching the word to the street sign.

He was cheating on her. The son of a bitch was having an affair. She couldn't believe it. It wasn't true. It had to be true. She had seen him kiss another woman with her very own eyes. How much more proof did she need?

~

A car was leaving just as Grace pulled up in front of Miller's. Somehow, she managed to park her car and accompany Caroline into the store. Somehow, she was able to find the words to greet the owner, Mrs. Pinkerton, without breaking into deep wracking sobs or throwing herself into the woman's arms. Mercifully, neither Caroline nor Mrs. Pinkerton seemed to notice the tremor in her voice. Caroline was too excited about the fitting;

Mrs. Pinkerton was deaf in one ear and couldn't hear much of anything.

A tiny, ancient woman, Mrs. Pinkerton had inherited the shop from her parents and outfitted everyone in the county who'd ever worn a riding habit, including Grace and Emma Rae. She'd always doted on the King girls, and Caroline was no exception. She immediately whisked her upstairs to try on her riding habit, while Grace hid her face in a rack of riding jackets and struggled to regain her composure.

"Honey, come look and see if this is all right," Mrs. Pinkerton called down to her a few minutes later.

A part of her was still outside in the car, watching Eddie whisper in the woman's ear, a gesture so intimate and familiar that she could almost hear what he was saying. Another part was dutifully dragging herself up the worn wooden steps to the fitting room, which Mrs. Pinkerton hadn't changed a bit in all the years since Grace was Caroline's age.

Grace almost gasped when she saw Caroline standing in front of the three-way mirror.

"That must take you back," said Mrs. Pinkerton, pinning the back of the jacket.

Dressed in an elegant black riding habit, Caroline looked like a beautiful grown woman trapped in the body of a child. Grace momentarily forgot her misery and gave herself over to the pleasure of seeing Caroline take a small step forward into adulthood.

"Please, can I get the boots?" said Caroline, abruptly bringing her back to reality.

They'd been over this territory before, almost as often as they'd argued about Caroline riding Possum versus Miss Lily.

"Honey, they're so expensive, and your little feet are going to grow so much!" Grace said, her resolve faltering.

As if she could sense that her mother was starting to waver, Caroline pressed on. "But why spend all that money on the suit and then chintz out on the boots?"

Grace was tempted to say yes, all right. She wanted to buy her the boots, if only to mitigate the pain she would suffer because Eddie had betrayed them. But his sin shouldn't have to be on her conscience. If anyone needed to make amends, it was Eddie.

"Can I use your phone?" she asked, too angry now to postpone the inevitable confrontation.

Mrs. Pinkerton pointed to the back of the shop. "In the office, there."

"Why do we always have to call Daddy when we want to buy something?" whined Caroline.

Grace refused to dignify the question other than to frown at her daughter before she marched next door to have it out with Eddie.

"You should have seen your mama and your

aunt Emma Rae when they were your age," said Mrs. Pinkerton, fussing with the sleeve of Caroline's jacket.

"Did they get to ride whoever they wanted?" Caroline asked.

"Oh, yes!" Mrs. Pinkerton smiled with fond recollection. "Your granddaddy would put them on any big ol' thing, and they would just ride their little hearts out."

"I knew it," Caroline said triumphantly, stockpiling this new piece of ammunition for the next skirmish in the war over Possum. She preened as she stared in the mirror and saw herself reflected there, wearing her new habit and boots, riding Possum to first place in the Winter National Youth Jumper Classic.

~

Mrs. Pinkerton's small, neatly furnished office doubled as a pictorial gallery of local horsemanship. Her walls were decorated with framed photographs of many of the riders she'd dressed in her forty-odd years at the store alongside their favorite horses. As Grace picked up the phone, she found one of her father, seated on the horse that had sired Ransom. Another was of herself and Emma Rae, in matching habits and pigtails, holding their horses' reins and grinning at the camera.

Grace didn't remember Mrs. Pinkerton taking the picture, but she did remember the habits,

Christmas presents from her parents when she was eight and Emma Rae was five. She had loved the jacket and pants so much she had worn them to bed for a week instead of pajamas, until Emma Rae told on her to their mother, and Georgia had scolded her for being such a silly girl.

That was the same year she'd discovered *Black Beauty* and Walter Farley. The year she decided she wanted to be either a jockey or a veterinarian when she grew up. She squinted at the picture to see what she was wearing on her feet. Mrs. Pinkerton was an enthusiastic equestrian chronicler, but an imperfect photographer. The picture was slightly out of focus, too fuzzy for her to determine what material the boots were made of.

She closed her eyes, and unexpectedly, a memory came back—of Wyly promising to buy her the pair of leather boots she coveted if she won first prize in the summer Youth Classic. Her horse had stumbled on the last rail, and she'd placed second. She'd cried herself to sleep for nights afterward, mourning the boots even more than the race.

She had been nine that summer, a year older than Caroline. She wondered whose pain she was hoping to salve with a pair of boots.

Her hands were shaking as she dialed Eddie's number. She endured two rings and was about to hang up when the receptionist answered. "Bichon Partners."

"Eddie Bichon's office, please," she said, sinking into Mrs. Pinkerton's chair.

She sent her husband a silent message: *Be there, Or else.*

"Eddie Bichon's office," said Eddie's secretary, an unfailingly cheerful middle-aged woman who didn't seem to mind having to pick up Eddie's dry cleaning or doing any of his other myriad private errands.

"Hello, June. It's Grace. Can I speak to Eddie?" she said. Her voice sounded thin and reedy in her ears.

"Miz Bichon, he's not in. He said he'd be at a meeting for the rest of the afternoon."

She tried to read June's tone. What did she know? Was it pity for a wife betrayed that was oozing out between the cracks of what the loyal secretary would permit herself to say?

"Did he say where?" she asked as casually as possible.

"No, ma'am, he sure didn't. If he calls in, you want me to have him call you?"

Grace pictured Eddie lying naked next to the young woman in some hotel bed, picking up a message that she'd tried to reach him.

"No," she said. She definitely did not want him to call her. She slammed down the phone and went to buy Caroline a pair of ridiculously expensive leather boots.

~

She stumbled through the rest of the day on automatic pilot. No one watching her would have guessed that her heart was shattering into tiny, poisonous, sharp-edged fragments of fury, grief, contempt, spite. She shoved her feelings into a recess deep below the surface of her consciousness and proceeded to carry on as if her world weren't flying apart at its core. As if watching her husband embrace another woman were a normal, everyday event for her.

She and Caroline were halfway through dinner when she realized she hadn't even checked the answering machine to see whether Eddie had been planning to join them. Not that she gave a damn. She sure as hell wasn't about to feed him. The bastard could fend for himself.

She pushed away her untouched plate of food, went over to the counter, and switched on the machine. Impatiently fast-forwarding through the tape, she listened to each message just long enough to catch the gist.

". . . so I need help testing recipes for the cookbook. Besides, I've gained ten pounds . . ." That was Lucy, who must have called early that morning before the meeting.

Sheila Mack was next: "I thought you might ask some of your Charity League friends if they'd be presenters for the Grand Prix. They've got the gowns."

She pressed fast-forward, then stopped in the middle of Emma Rae's message about Have a Heart. ". . . some kind of deal, the guy was asking five, but the horse is being sold as part of a divorce settlement, so Dad's got him down to the low twos. What can I say, Grace? Daddy's an asshole, big surprise. I'll call you if I find out anything else."

Slices of her life, taped sound bites that didn't seem to add up to much of anything. She fast-forwarded again, pressed play, and found a message from Eddie.

". . . Dad wants me to go out to dinner with these clients, so I'll be home by eleven. Kiss the doodlebug for me. Bye."

She rewound to the beginning of the message. "Hey, Grace. It's me," he said. "This meeting took longer than we thought, and now Dad wants me to—"

She cut him off, not wanting to hear the lie twice. As she reset the tape, she glanced at Caroline, who was staring dreamily at some image that she alone could see as she picked at her food. She was quietly talking to herself, in that way that only children often do, supplying both sides of the dialogue running through her brain.

Poor Caroline. They had always meant to give her a brother or sister, but the moment had never seemed quite right. They had ignored the issue for so long that the question of why they had put off the decision had begun to take on a life of its own, a presence that Grace circled warily as she moved around the house.

Maybe she shouldn't have been so careful to avoid it. Maybe not making a decision about the second child somehow had led Eddie into the arms of another woman. Or maybe it wouldn't have mattered one damn bit either way. Maybe Eddie was just one of those men she'd always pitied other women for marrying.

~

She couldn't think of anything to do but wait for him to come home, she she got into bed at an absurdly early hour for a Friday night and pretended to read a magazine. A couple of hours later, Caroline appeared in her nightgown and the new riding boots, whimpering that she had had a bad dream and wanted to snuggle. Glad for the company, Grace pulled back the covers and tucked her into Eddie's side of the bed.

She watched her daughter's breath begin to flow in a slow, even rhythm as she relaxed into sleep. One arm was folded under her head, the other flung out with the palm turned upward, as if she were waiting for someone to take her hand. Grace ran her fingers across Caroline's open palm, tracing her lifeline to where it met her index finger.

Asleep, she looked utterly peaceful and content.

She'd wanted to stay up to show Eddie her boots, but Grace had told her no, Daddy would be out until late. She had asked Grace to make sure Daddy kissed her good night when he came home. Of course, Grace said, picturing the woman in the red crepe suit as she'd leaned in with her mouth to meet Eddie's lips.

She picked up her magazine again and flipped through the pages, all the while listening for Eddie's car to pull into the driveway. The image of Edna's tennis bracelet, supposedly a bribe from her errant husband, popped into her mind. What was it Lucy had said? *If that's the way it works, that puts us in the running for the Hope Diamond.*

Us. The implication hit her like a fist in the belly. Today wasn't the first time Eddie had cheated on her. It was just the first time she'd caught him at it. Lucy had all but admitted she knew Eddie was involved with another woman . . . or was it *women*? How many had there been? How long had this been going on? Who else knew, besides Lucy? Or was she the only one who didn't know?

She looked at the clock: ten:fifty-nine. What a fool she'd been, believing his stories about business dinners and late-night meetings. A stupid, naive fool, sitting home like a good girl while her husband was out screwing around.

The numbers on the clock flipped to eleven. She jumped out of bed. The hell with it. She couldn't sit here anymore and wait for him to show up. She had no idea where she was going or what she was going to do when she got there. She only knew it was going to take a damn sight more than a tennis bracelet to set things right again.

~

Caroline was confused but excited by the novelty of getting up in the middle of the night to go driving through the darkened streets of town. Where were they going, she kept asking her mother. All Grace would tell her was, "Never mind. You'll see." They must be having an adventure, she decided. Perhaps they were on a treasure hunt. Why else would her mother keep staring into the night, as if she were searching for something or someone?

She smothered a yawn and flattened her nose against the window. "Hey! That's Daddy's car," she shouted, pointing across the street at Eddie's Mercedes, which was parked in a lot next to a bar.

Grace rolled up in front of the bar. She strained to see through the big picture window that faced the street, but the glare of the streetlights obscured her view. She double-parked her jeep, turned on her flashers, and got out of the car.

"Wait here, sweetie," she told Caroline.

Past caring that she was dressed only in her nightgown, she marched up to the window and peered inside. She was almost please to find Eddie, his arm around the woman in the red crepe suit. They were seated at a crowded table, along with some of his friends and several women, all of whom looked young enough to still be in college.

Unmindful as always of her mother's instructions, Caroline had gotten out of the car and come to join Grace. She tugged at her mother's sleeve, but Grace was oblivious to her presence. She knocked on the window and yelled, "Eddie! I can see you!"

Caroline grinned. So this was the game! She wanted to play, too. "Hi, Daddy! Hi!" she shouted, rapping her fist against the glass.

Her voice shocked Grace out of her stupor. "Ladybug! Get back in the car!" she ordered.

By now, their banging had succeeded in rousing the interest of most of the patrons, including Eddie, who suddenly realized that the crazy lady outside with the kid was his wife.

"Uh-oh," one of his pals said. "You're busted, buddy."

"Get your ass out here now!" Grace screamed, so loudly that Eddie could hear the words through the thick pane of glass.

"Jesus H. Christ," he muttered, getting up and heading for the exit.

His friends grinned. "Yep. He was crucified, too," said a second.

Eddie shot out the door like a torpedo and stormed over to Grace, who had scooped Caroline up in her embrace, as if to shield them both from his anger.

"What in the name of God are you doin', Grace? Have you lost your mind?" he yelled.

"Hi, Daddy! We came to get you," Caroline sang out.

He kissed her cheek as he lifted her out of Grace's arms. "Hey, tadpole. Let me put you in the car."

He brought her over to the jeep and gently deposited her in the back seat. Then he angrily retraced his steps. "Now, Grace, get in the goddamn car!" he ordered her.

Grace glowered at him. "No," she said.

"You are making a spectacle of yourself! Now, get in!" He grabbed her arm and tried to pull her around to the driver's side of the jeep.

She jerked free of his graps. "No! No! *You're* making a spectacle of me!" she shouted, clenching her fists to stop herself from hitting him.

"What in the hell is wrong with you?" he demanded.

She hated him now even more for lying. He was trying to make her out to be the bad guy, the wacko who was causing the trouble. How stupid did he think she was? "I saw you," she said coldly.

Eddie shook his head. "What are you talking about?"

His innocent expression was so transparent that she would have laughed if she hadn't wanted so badly to cry. "I saw you," she said, lowering her voice so that Caroline couldn't hear her. "On the corner of Fifth and Union. You know what I'm talking about. I saw you. With a girl in a red crepe suit. The girl that's in there."

"Honey, I don't know what you saw, but it wasn't me," he said. He extended his hand to her as if his touch were proof enough that he was telling the truth.

She stared at him in disbelief. "You mean that's it? That's all I get? You're just going to stand here and lie to me in the middle of the street?"

He was caught, and they both knew it. "What? What do you want me to say?" He shrugged, which only made her more furious. She thought, *How about "sorry," for starters?* But it wasn't her job to give him lessons in how to save the marriage he'd so easily sabotaged.

"I want you to say good-bye to Caroline," she told him, calmer now that she'd forced a showdown.

"Where're you goin'?" he demanded as she walked past him to get into the car.

She didn't have to answer him. It had obviously been quite a while since he'd told her the truth about where he was going.

"Home to Daddy?" he taunted her.

She walked back around to the front of the car and said something she never would have imagined saying to her husband. "Fuck you, Eddie."

Out of the corner of her eye, she noticed that a crowd of people had gathered at the window inside the bar. They were staring at her and Eddie, gawking shamelessly as if they were watching a program on television.

Caroline, who had climbed into the front seat, was also staring at them with a look that bordered on terror. Grace rolled down her window. "Kiss Daddy good-bye, angel," she said.

"I'll see you later, alligator," Eddie said, leaning in to give her a hug.

"After a while, alliga . . ." She quickly corrected her herself. "I mean crocodile."

She kept her head turned, her gaze fixed on him as Grace started the car and drove away. When she could no longer see him, she turned back to her mother. "Mama? Is Daddy in trouble?" she asked timidly.

Grace reached over and squeezed her hand, which felt damp and cold. "Yes, baby. He is," she said. "Daddy is in very big trouble."

3

Wyly had already turned off the light and was about to get into bed when he heard what sounded like car tires crunching along the gravel road that ran past his house, then continuing down the driveway toward the converted carriage house where Emma Rae lived. He didn't usually make a habit of spying on his daughter, but midnight seemed a mite late for someone—even someone like Emma Rae—to be receiving callers.

Through his bedroom window, which faced the front of Emma Rae's house, he saw Grace's jeep gliding past with the headlights turned off. As he was wondering why she'd come sneaking in to pay her sister a visit at this strange hour, Georgia padded over and slipped herself into the circle of his arms.

He motioned with his head for her to follow his gaze. They watched Grace lift Caroline out of the car and carry her over to Emma Rae, who was waiting for them in her open doorway. Grace put her finger to her lips, as if she were telling Emma Rae to be quiet.

"Oh, Lord." Georgia whispered as her daughters disappeared into Emma Rae's house.

Grace was not the type of girl to go gadding about in the middle of the night, especially not with Caroline in tow. Georgia could only guess at the significance of the tableau she'd just witnessed. But it was an educated guess, one that kept her awake long after Wyly was snoring in his sleep while she sadly contemplated the hurts men and women inflicted on each other, all in the name of love.

~

As Georgia tossed and turned in her bed, and Caroline lay asleep in Emma Rae's guest room, Grace was slumped on the sofa, weepily describing the events of the afternoon and evening. It took her a while to choke out the whole awful story, beginning from the moment she'd seen Eddie kissing the woman in the red crepe suit.

Emma Rae sat at the other end of the sofa, gaping at her sister as if Grace had just told her she'd been abducted by aliens. Her thick brown hair flew from side to side as she kept shaking her head and handing Grace one tissue after another to mop up her endless stream of tears. She couldn't help but smirk at the idea of Grace in her nightgown, cursing out Eddie in front of his bimbo and the rest of his friends. She wished she had been there to see it herself.

That skunk Eddie! She slammed her glass down on the coffee table with such force that water splashed over the sides. The noise woke up her dog Hoover, a big yellow creature with doleful eyes who'd been napping under the table. He raised his head to register his irritation and snuffled in protest before settling back down to sleep.

Finally, Grace ran out of words and lapsed into a dark, brooding silence. Emma Rae sighed. She had never believed that Grace and Eddie had the perfect marriage. Was there any such thing? But Eddie was basically a good guy, and Caroline was a terrific kid, and Emma Rae had always been just a little bit envious of her big sister's good fortune. And grateful, too, because she figured she had learned from Grace's mistakes what choices not to make.

She felt a deep well of sympathy for all Grace had been through today. Eddie better hope they didn't cross paths any time soon. She was so mad at him for hurting Grace that she was just aching to smack that gorgeous conceited face of his.

"Well, this is just an unholy mess," she said. "And the timing . . . Right in the middle of this goddamn Wheeler Farm deal with Eddie and his dad. If you're expecting any loyalty from Daddy right now . . ."

"I'm not! Believe me!" Grace said bitterly. "I'm not completely deluded. Besides, it wasn't a business decision for Chrissake! I mean, I *saw* the son of a bitch!"

Emma Rae shook her head. Grace, like her parents, was an expert at ignoring the truth, even when it was staring her smack in the eyes. "Well, Grace, what a fucking news flash! I've always worried about something like this happening."

"Really?" Grace glared at her sister. So Lucy *wasn't* the only one to know that Eddie had been unfaithful to her. "Well, if you were so goddamn worried, why in the hell didn't you say something?"

"What am I supposed to say? You marry a guy whose nickname in college is Hound Dog. What'd you think was going to happen?"

Good old Emma. She never could keep her damn mouth shut. "Emma Rae! Do you always have to be so goddamn insensitive? You don't think I feel like an idiot? I mean, I'm out there in the goddamn street. What am I supposed to do? Look at me! Jesus. I mean . . . what?" She almost started to cry again, but she was too angry . . . at Eddie, Emma Rae, most of all herself.

Emma Rae scooted across the sofa and threw her arms around Grace. "No, you did the right thing. You did. I'm proud of you," she assured her.

It was a small consolation, but she was feeling too wretched to reject whatever shred of comfort was offered. She struggled not to break down again. Her eyes were already raw and swollen from crying. She leaned her head against Emma Rae's shoulder, thankful that she had her sister there to turn to. "I'm gonna kill the son of a bitch," she said softly.

~

The light was just beginning to deepen from palest violet to blue when Emma Rae pulled herself out of bed and stumbled into the kitchen to make coffee. She hated getting up early and had to fight every morning to obey the summons of her alarm clock. But her effort was well worth the reward: an hour or two of blessed solitude when the hush of dawn was broken only by the birds chirping overhead and the horses whinnying in the barn.

Some mornings, she sat at the pine table in the kitchen and caught up on her paperwork. Running the auction arm of the family business was hardly what she'd expected to be doing at age twenty-five. But the job was fascinating and the pay was good, and she was prepared to stay for as long as she and her father could get along without knocking heads.

Living in the carriage house also had its advantages. She was welcome next door for dinner whenever she didn't feel like fixing her own, and she got to enjoy the surrounding beauty of the King Farms without actually having to share a roof with her parents.

Today, as she often did on fine mornings, she took her coffee outside and curled up on the porch swing to savor the stillness before the coming storm. She didn't need a crystal ball to predict that Wyly was going to have a fit as soon as he found out about Grace and Eddie. She could hear him now, as clearly as if he were standing right in front of her: "We've never had a divorce in this family, and I'm not about to tolerate one now."

She grinned. There was so much her father wouldn't tolerate from his women. It was a mercy he didn't have them all in corsets and hoops.

A pickup truck and trailer were parked in front of the barn. She guessed the truck belonged to Jamie Johnson, who must have arrived way before sunrise. Curious to see the famous horse that was causing so much trouble, she walked around to the side of the house and almost burst out laughing. Jamie Johnson was walking Have a Heart, showing him off to a group of interested onlookers that included several of the grooms and one little girl dressed in a nightgown and leather riding boots.

Two things were for certain. Caroline was very much Grace's daughter. And Have a Heart was one magnificent horse. Even in the dim light of dawn, she could see his long black legs and deep brown coat. He was dark and handsome, much like his former owner. She leaned against the porch rail and took a sip of coffee. Yes, indeed, she thought. This could well be a Grand Prix that none of them would never forget.

~

She went to rouse Grace, then showered and quickly got dressed. The next time she checked the view from her window, Wyly had appeared in the yard. He and Caroline were standing a few yards away from the other men; Caroline, quite obviously mimicking Grace, was reenacting for him her parents' fight.

"Grace you better get it together. Daddy's gonna be here in about ten seconds," Emma Rae yelled.

"Oh, shit!" Grace mumbled from the other room, as her feet hit the floor.

Emma Rae watched Caroline run off to see her grandmother while Wyly headed for the carriage house. A minute later, he was knocking on her door, not waiting for her to open it before he barged right in.

"Hey, Daddy, here's your schedule," she said brightly. "The Troutman auction is at noon. I'm meeting Mr. Yopp about the financing at four, so don't be late."

Wyly glanced around for Grace. "What in the Sam Hell is going on here?" he growled.

"What're you talkin' about?" she asked, fully aware of how unconvincing she sounded.

"Honey, if you want to succeed in business, you're gonna have to learn to lie a whole lot better than that," he said as Grace strolled into the living room, wearing a falsely cheerful expression that convinced no one.

"Hey, Daddy." She waved at him wanly.

Wyly shot Emma Rae a look whose meaning was clear: *Scram!*

Behind Wyly's back, she sent Grace a silent message of courage and concern. "I'm gonna go see about some stuff," she said reluctantly, and left them alone to have it out.

Wyly wasted no time. "In your goddamn nightgown? Is that part true?" he demanded.

"Daddy—" She put out her hands, a gesture of supplication.

"Is that how you behave in front of your child? What in the name of God has gotten into you?"

Emma Rae had warned her not to depend on him for support. How often had she smiled to hear Wyly say that Eddie was like a son to him? But wasn't she still just as much as his daughter? "Daddy, please," she said.

"You think you're invisible?"

In the morning light, she could see that there might have been other ways to deal with the situation. But if anyone owed an explanation for his behavior, it was Eddie. "We're having some problems," she said lamely.

"We? Who we? He wasn't in his goddamn underwear, was he?"

She shook her head. "No. I meant—"

"How the hell is you running around town nekked gonna solve anything? You trying to humiliate your whole goddamn family? Do you know what your mother is gonna say?"

In her place, Emma Rae would have known how to protect herself from Wyly's wrath and the threat of her mother's disapproval. Even as a small child, she had amazed Grace with her fearless ability to challenge their father. He was always so damn sure he was right—just like Emma Rae. But if ever she had known she was right, it was this one time. As miserable as she felt, she didn't much care whether or not Wyly agreed with her.

~

While Caroline was occupied with setting the dining room table for breakfast, Georgia, Emma Rae, and Eula, the housekeeper, were keeping a vigil for Grace by the kitchen window.

"Oh, my God. Her heart must be in a million little pieces," Georgia said quietly, staring across the distance between the two houses.

Emma Rae helped herself to another cup of coffee and brusquely tried to set Georgia straight. "No, her pride. Now, for God's sake, don't get maudlin."

But Georgia's heart was aching for her older daughter. "It's just too awful! I can't believe he would do that! What was he thinking of?"

"Probably the same thing he was thinking

with," Emma Rae said with a smirk. She winked at Eula, waiting for Georgia to get the point.

Georgia sighed. "Don't be vulgar, Emma Rae," she said.

Emma Rae's frequent use of off-color language was an ongoing point of conflict between them. Georgia firmly believed that a lady didn't have to resort to coarseness in order to express herself. She adored both her daughters, but there was so much she didn't understand about Emma Rae. Though both girls had Wyly's darker coloring, they had inherited her distinctive features. Why, just last week, Frank Lewis, the family doctor, had commented that the King women were clearly from the same gene pool.

But the resemblance between herself and Emma Rae was skin-deep. Emma Rae was a free spirit who insisted on charting her own unique course, no matter how unexplored or troubling the waters might be. Though Wyly scoffed at her fears that Emma Rae would wind up an old maid, Georgia often worried that she didn't even have a beau, at least none that Georgia was aware of. She suspected that men were put off by her daughter's candor and independent ways. On the other hand, there was Grace, who had always been the perfect wife and lady, crying her eyes out next door because Eddie was temporarily not in his right mind.

She gave Eula and Emma Rae a warning look as Caroline came skipping into the kitchen to get the silverware. "Spoons on the right or the left?" she asked her grandmother.

Eager to resume their discussion, the women responded in a chorus, "On the right."

"And for Grace to humiliate herself like that!" Georgia clucked after Caroline had left the room. She pulled out a loaf of bread and began laying slices on the rack of the toaster oven. "I just can't stand the thought of it! What in the world are we going to do now?"

It seemed to Emma Rae that aside from not making Grace feel even worse than she already did, there wasn't much the family *could* do. Her sister wasn't the first person in the county to embarrass herself in public, and she sure as hell wouldn't be the last. People would talk about her for maybe a week or two until someone else did something dumb or crazy or illegal, and then everybody would forget all about Grace Bichon.

The point would be lost on Georgia. "Whatever it is, I'm sure it will be hopelessly ineffective," Emma Rae said.

Eula shook a spoon at her. "Miss Smart."

"Well, I'm going back over there. She's probably had all she can take." Emma Rae grabbed a piece of Eula's coffee cake and was gone.

Georgia moved back to the window and saw Wyly emerge from the carriage house. He and Emma Rae walked across the yard toward each other like a couple of Wild West gunslingers at high noon—two kindred souls, too much alike for their own good, it sometimes seemed to Georgia. They almost passed without speaking when they met midway between the two houses, but then they did stop.

Georgia rolled her eyes at Eula. "Oh, God. Here we go."

~

Emma Rae stared at a point on the horizon beyond her father's right profile. "You get her all squared away?" she asked.

"She'll be all right," said Wyly, gazing down at his feet as he dug a hole in the ground with his boot.

"She say what was going on?"

Wyly shrugged. "Just a fight."

Emma Rae snorted. As usual, it was left to her to fill in the blanks. "Eddie's fucking somebody else," she said, using the language she knew her father would best understand.

She sneaked a peek at his expression, saw that he didn't even flinch. "That for sure?" he asked, still examining the ground beneath his feet.

"Yup," she answered in kind.

"Okay. See you at noon," he said.

Emma Rae turned and watched him walk back to the main house. He didn't fool her for a second. She knew he cared. She had figured that out a long time ago. The question was, when was he going to figure it out for himself?

~

"I thought we'd decided I was going to talk to her first," Georgia scolded as soon as Wyly came stomping into the kitchen.

Wyly grinned and planted a kiss on her cheek. "Well, I guess I lied," he said and headed into the dining room. He was ready for breakfast; he felt as if he had already done a day's work.

"I mean it, Wyly!"

She swatted his behind as he marched past her. There was no stopping Wyly once he set his mind to something. He was incorrigible. Always had been. Always would be. She wouldn't have had him any other way.

~

The phone in her office rang three times before Grace found the energy to answer it. She hit the speakerphone button. "King Farms," she said, then cradled her head in her hands.

Her best friend's voice, sounding slightly frantic, filled the room. "Grace, it's Luce. I'm trying to make this damn hazelnut buttercream, and it looks weird."

"Like what?" Grace said automatically. Lucy wasn't that good an actress. The news about her fight with Eddie must not have spread very far, or Lucy would be asking about a lot more than buttercream.

"Like grainy and like it's going to separate."

Her head ached, and a lump the size of a watermelon seemed to have lodged itself in her throat. She had hardly slept a wink all night. When she had finally dropped off, she'd dreamed that Eddie had been arrested for stealing Ransom and selling him to the girl in the red crepe suit.

But the world hadn't stopped just because Eddie had lost his mind. "It said, 'Cream softened butter and sugar'?"

"I did that," said Lucy.

Lucy had many wonderful talents. Baking wasn't one of them. "Did you melt the butter in the microwave to soften it?"

Her question was followed by a long pause. She almost smiled as she broke the silence. "You did, didn't you?"

"Shit," Lucy said succinctly.

"Start over," Grace advised her.

Lucy's sigh was loud and heartfelt. " 'Bye," she said.

Grace hung up the phone and echoed Lucy's sigh. If only her biggest problem right now were a grainy buttercream icing. She was tempted to call Lucy back to ask her what she knew about Eddie that she wasn't telling. Her pride kept her from dialing the number. She still wasn't prepared to hear, even from Lucy, that he'd been living up to his college nickname.

She glanced out her window. Hank was in the training ring, riding Ransom, who was taking one jump after another with a long, powerful stride. Through the open door of her office, she could hear her father chatting with Jamie Johnson, whom she recognized from his previous visits to the farm and other Grand Prix competitions.

"That horse is one scopey son of a gun. That's for sure," said Jamie, sounding genuinely impressed.

"Well, don't you worry about him," Wyly said.

Grace shook her head. Wyly was wrong about so many things: about shortchanging Ransom, who was going to give Jamie's horse a run for his money, if she had anything to say about it. About putting the blame on her instead of Eddie.

"Honey?" As if to keep her from getting too worked up about Wyly, Georgia suddenly appeared in the doorway, her arms loaded with ledgers and checkbooks. "Hi. I thought we should get caught up on the books here before it gets any crazier."

She had been expecting her mother to show up. She would have been surprised if she hadn't. But the last thing she needed now was a pep talk from Georgia. "Mother. Now's not a good time." She pointed to the stack of papers on her desk. "All our entries have to be at the show office before five."

"Well, then, just give me the accounts, and I'll

enter everything." Georgia sat down and tried to arrange her face so that she didn't look absolutely worried sick about her daughter.

"Mom—"

Georgia's blue eyes filled with tears. "Honey, he slipped," she said.

"Mother, please, I don't want to talk about this with you!"

"Honey, it happens in the best of marriages. It doesn't mean he doesn't love you. The decisions you make now, you'll have to live with for the rest of your life. And so will Caroline."

Grace picked up her pen, hoping Georgia would take the hint and leave. She couldn't bear to listen to a defense of Eddie's behavior. Not now . . . not from her own mother. Bad enough that Wyly had taken his side. But she expected more from her mother.

"Are you through?" she said coldly.

Georgia refused to be derailed from her mission. Still clutching the ledgers, she leaned forward across the desk. "You have a child who loves her daddy. And he loves her. And God knows you cannot let one little slip take all that away. Now, he slipped, and as crazy as it seems, it's up to you to help him up."

"I don't believe I'm hearing this." Grace put her hands over her ears, the gesture of a small child who couldn't bear to listen to her mother's well-intentioned lecture. She was relieved when her mother got up to go. But Georgia wasn't finished yet.

"And I'll tell you something else," she said. "You've gone about this in a way that everyone's going to be talking about for a long time. Well, you let them talk, but from now on, this is private family business. You just keep your head up and smile. Don't give them the satisfaction. You need to talk, you come to me."

She stood in the middle of the room as if she were waiting for Grace's response. Grace was too angry to speak. She pressed her lips together tightly, afraid of what might otherwise come spilling out. Her parents had this whole thing twisted around, so that *she* was the one who had behaved badly. It was so unfair! All her life, she'd been a good girl and done what was expected of her. They had set high standards, and she'd met them, over and over again. Didn't she deserve their loyalty and understanding, if only this one time?

Georgia smiled. "We'll do the books another time. I love you, honey," she said, and then she was finally gone.

~

The day stretched on and on. Grace felt as if it would never end. Every time the phone rang, she was sure it would be Eddie calling to apologize. But it was always someone else, and she wasn't sure whether she was relieved or disappointed not to hear his voice at the other end. Didn't he care? Did she matter so little to him that he didn't even want to try and patch things up?

She yearned to cry and scream and give in to the pain, but the Grand Prix forms had to be filled out by the end of the afternoon, and there was no one else who could do them. She swallowed aspirins for her headache and forced herself to concentrate. The noises—of the horses snorting in their stalls, the grooms calling to one another, her father leading Jamie on a tour of the barn—all receded into the background as she buried herself in the endless, mind-numbing questions on the forms.

She finished with time enough to drive over to show headquarters and file the entries, including one for Ransom. She was taking a risk by contradicting Wyly's wishes, but she still might get him to change his mind. She didn't much care if he was angry with her. What much worse could he say than what he'd already said this morning?

She had just arrived back at Emma Rae's house and had gone to get a glass of water when she heard Emma Rae yelling at her from the living room. "Grace!" she called excitedly. "Eddie's coming."

"What?" She stepped out of the kitchen and stared at Emma Rae like a deer caught in a car's headlights.

"Daddy must've called him. What do you want me to do? Do you want to talk to him?"

She shook her head. "No! I don't know!" Her hand flew to her hair. She must look a mess. She didn't want him to see her like this. "Where in the hell is Caroline?"

"Mom took her over to Aunt Rae's," Emma Rae said, keeping an eye on Eddie through the window.

"Thank God. Well, he knows I'm here." She grabbed her purse. "Keep him busy for a second!" she called over her shoulder as she rushed into the bedroom to comb her hair and put on fresh lipstick.

Emma Rae waited for Eddie to knock, then took her time opening the door. She folded her arms across her chest and deliberately blocked the view into the house. His expression was the perfect blend of humility and concern. She didn't buy it, not for a moment.

"Is she here?" he asked, dodging past her to slip inside.

"Yeah," she said, lowering her voice conspiratorially.

Eddie grinned, as if to say, I *knew* you'd be on my side.

Emma Rae kneed him hard in the groin. His smile abruptly disappeared as he howled and dropped to the floor.

She smiled. "I'll get her," she said graciously. She strolled across the room and tapped on the bedroom door. "Grace?" she called. "The lying cheating sack of shit is here." She leaned against the wall a few feet away from her brother-in-law and contendedly watched him moaning and writing in agony.

Grace opened the door, looked around, but didn't see him. "Where?" she said.

A strange noise—the grunt of an animal in pain—drew her eyes across the room. She found Eddie curled in a ball, his hands tucked tightly between his legs. "Oh my God!" she screamed. She ran over and knelt by his side. "Emma Rae? What did you do?"

Emma Rae barely smothered her grin. "You said keep him busy. He's busy holding his nuts."

"Goddamn it!" Eddie swore. He struggled to his knees and glared at Emma Rae.

"Eddie? Are you all right?" Grace asked anxiously.

"No, goddamnit!" he gasped, still trying to catch his breath.

"Help me get him up!" Grace urged her sister.

"No!" Eddie shouted at Emma Rae. "You just stay the fuck over there!"

"Don't worry. I wouldn't walk that far to help you up."

As furious as she was with Eddie, Grace was horrified by what her sister had done. "Oh my God! Emma Rae, what is wrong with you?"

"Consider it a blow for your dignity." Emma Rae smirked at her.

Grace was so close to tears that she could hardly

speak. "What's dignified about kicking somebody in the balls?"

"Well, *I* feel better."

"Jesus Christ, Emma," Eddie exploded as he finally pulled himself to his feet.

"Really, Em. That was totally uncalled-for!" Grace chastised her in the same severe tone she normally reserved for Caroline's very worst misdeeds.

It finally dawned on Emma Rae that Grace was genuinely upset with her. "Well, it's done now," she said contritely.

But Grace was not about to let her off the hook so easily. Her insides were churning with rage: at Eddie, herself, her parents, now even Emma Rae. She was overwhelmed with exhaustion and confusion and a burning desire to allay even a small measure of her pain by meting out punishment.

She had taught Caroline that hitting people was unacceptable, even if they hit her first. She didn't believe in corporal punishment. She had never so much as spanked her daughter. Now, she said, "I think you should let Eddie punch you in the arm."

Eddie gaped at her. "I don't want to punch her," he said, trying to recover his dignity. "At least not in the arm."

"Well, I want you to!" she said sharply. She gestured to her sister. "Emma Rae, get over here!"

The two of them exchanged glances, silently agreeing that crazy as it seemed, they may as well do as she'd said before she snapped and veered over the edge into total hysteria.

"Now, Eddie, punch her as hard as you want," Grace instructed him.

Emma Rae stuck out her arm and braced herself. Eddie whacked her with his fist. The force of his blow stunned both of them. She turned her head so neither he nor Grace could see her wince.

"C'mon, Ed. I didn't even feel that," she lied.

He scowled at her. "Well, I'm in a weakened state."

Grace was fast losing patience. "Now apologize," she told Emma Rae.

Emma Rae hesitated. She was about to object. He had paid her back. Eye for an eye, tooth for a tooth . . . Wasn't that enough? But Grace still looked and sounded as if she were on the verge of losing what little self-control she had left.

"I'm sorry," Emma Rae said grudgingly. "But not for the reasons you may think," she added. Then, fed up with the whole damn mess, she decided to leave them alone to work things out for themselves.

She hurried out of the house without saying good-bye. Grace felt a sudden flash of panic. She had been anticipating and dreading this moment all day. Now, she felt utterly lost. There was nothing he could possibly say that would heal her pain. She turned away, not wanting him to see her suffering. But he was her husband. She still loved him. Or did she?

"Grace." He came over, touched her arm.

"What?" she said, gritting her teeth. She refused to feel sorry for him. *She* was the victim of his stupidity. The pain belonged to her.

His fingers felt cold against her bare skin. She sensed his tension . . . and his fear. He wasn't good at expressing himself. He could tell a joke, make someone feel at ease in their home, laugh with friends. But conversation had never come easy for him. Talking about anything serious, especially feelings, always tied his tongue up in knots.

"Look, I know—" he began.

"No, you don't know!" She whirled around and glared at him. The words were the best he could do, but they were poorly chosen. "You *don't* know what it's like to be *lied* to, and you *don't* know what it's like to be sitting there with your child while you watch your husband making out with somebody on the street, and you don't know what it feels like to be made a big fat fucking fool of in front of everybody! So, please, do not begin with 'I know,' because you *do not know*."

Eddie exhaled sharply, as if he'd been holding his breath the whole time she'd been yelling at him. "What I was going to say," he began, speaking very carefully, "is that I know I'm one hundred percent in the wrong here, and I don't blame you for being mad."

"What a comfort," she said bitterly.

"Grace."

He was begging for forgiveness. She could see it in his eyes, hear it in his voice. He'd never done that before, not in all the years they'd been married. They argued, as every married couple did, about whose fault it was that they'd run out of toothpaste and whether they could afford to buy a new car and who had time to pick Caroline up from her tennis lesson. Sometimes, the fights got more serious; accusations that began with phrases like "You never . . ." or "You always . . ." flew between them. Occasionally, they would become so incensed with each other that they stopped speaking for a day or two.

Grace, even more than Eddie, suffered during those silences. She hated conflict. She invariably made the first move toward reconciliation. But not this time.

"I don't want this," she said. "I don't want to be this person, this *wife*! I feel like an idiot! Can you understand that?"

He stared at her, mute with guilt.

"What if Caroline had seen you? Do you know how close she came?" she demanded.

"I know. I'm sorry."

She believed him. Still, she said, "I don't care if you're sorry! I'm not that kind of woman, Eddie, that can just let it go. That was not our deal. I want you to leave now."

"Don't I get to say anything?" he asked, sounding almost annoyed with her.

He still hadn't grasped how badly he'd wronged her. He'd expected her to be softer. More understanding. She felt herself wavering, and said, "I'd really rather you didn't."

"Where's the doodlebug?" he said, frustrated about being so much in the wrong.

"She's not here," said Grace, feeling on slightly safer territory now. "She's with Mother."

"You can't stop me from seeing her, Grace!" He lashed out at her.

"I'm not! I didn't know you were coming! Don't make something out of nothing. She's at Aunt Rae's. If you want to see her, go over there. I dare you."

"Well, will you tell her I love her?" he asked.

He looked as close to crying as she'd ever seen him. Then she remembered him kissing the woman in the red crepe suit. "Whatever that means," she said coldly.

He looked at her as if he didn't recognize her. "Jesus," he said, shaking his head.

She'd asked him to leave, but now that he was moving towards the door, she felt the urge to hold him there until she was done pouring out every last iota of anger and hurt and resentment that she'd stored up over the past thirty-six hours. She wanted to rant and rave and demand to know why he had done this to them. How could he so carelessly destroy the marriage and family they'd built together? Didn't he get it? Didn't he understand anything at all about her?

"I mean, Christ, Eddie!" she said. "You don't even like horses!"

He slammed the door behind him and hurried to his car just as Emma Rae was walking back to her house. "Em," he called.

She walked right past him without saying a word. She knew that he wanted to talk to her about Grace, but she wasn't about to become his ally against her sister. As much as she hoped that Grace could find it in her heart to forgive Eddie, she had no taste for playing their go-between.

"Emma Rae!" Eddie yelled.

She turned to glance at him without breaking her stride. "Are you addressing me?"

"Yes!"

"Well," she said, rubbing the place on her arm where he'd hit her, "lick it, put a stamp on it, and mail it to someone who gives a shit."

4

~

Grace rarely felt prouder than when she saw Caroline sitting astride a horse, looking every bit the champion rider she was destined to be. Caroline was even more devoted to riding than Grace had been as a child, if such a thing were possible. She never seemed to mind getting up early to help with the horses or to take a lesson, and sleeping over at Emma Rae's just meant she could spend that much more time around the barn.

She was out of the house on Saturday morning long before either Emma Rae or Grace was awake. Grace got up, drank her coffee, then went to find Caroline to give her breakfast. She tracked her down at the paddock, where she was riding Miss Lily under Hank's careful supervision. Framed against the blue sky, child and horse made an exquisite picture: the fine-boned chestnut horse with the white star in the middle of her forehead and the socks on her hind feet guided through her paces by the beautiful, confident little girl whose honey-blond ponytail fluttered in the breeze.

Grace smiled. Whatever happened between herself and Eddie, nothing could spoil the joy she got from seeing her daughter grow and develop. She stood on the side and watched as Caroline slipped her boots into the stirrups.

"Okay, just trot around and warm up," he said after she had tightened the girth.

"Hey, sweetie plum!" Grace called out as Caroline passed by with her body squared and her seat well into the saddle.

"Hey," Caroline said glumly.

"Is she driving you crazy over Possum?" Grace asked Hank.

"Nope," he said gruffly, barely acknowledging her presence. "Keep her in a trot," he told Caroline, who was pushing Miss Lily toward a canter.

Caroline obediently decreased the pace and circled the paddock. "Hey, Possum," she greeted her favorite, trotting past the crosties where Possum was getting a bath.

"Lookin' good, sweetie!" Grace said when she came by again.

Caroline wrinkled her nose. "Bo-ring!" she announced.

Miss Lily had a quiet, sedate personality, especially compared to Possum. But she was an excellent jumper who would pop over anything put in front of her. Her experience in previous competitions had taught her to stay calm and approach the jumps with a calm, easy stride. All of which made her, in Grace's opinion, the perfect mount for Caroline's first Grand Prix.

"Slow her just a tad," Hank said, keeping his back to Grace.

It dawned on her then that both her daughter and the trainer were doing their best to ignore her this morning. She realized she had some fence-mending to do, especially with Hank, who seemed to be blaming her for Wyly's bad judgment. "Hank, look," she said uncomfortably. "I've been waiting for the right opportunity to bring it up with Dad. But you have to know if it was up to me—"

He cut her off with a dismissive wave. "But it's not, is it?" he said, his voice sour with disappointment. "Look, Grace, I'm not gonna leave before the event, so don't worry about it. Unlike some people, I take a certain pride in keeping my word. But when it's over, I'm gone. Now, I've got work to do."

He walked away before she had a chance to tell him she'd filed an entry form for him and Ransom. A moment later, Caroline trotted past yet again and didn't even bother to glance her way.

A phrase from high school Latin danced through her brain: *persona non grata*. An unacceptable or unwelcome person. Well, at least she knew what she was—and in a foreign language, no less. It was great to have an identity. She sighed and walked around the barn to the paddock to take a look at Wyly's new horse.

She instantly understood why her father had Harvey, as Jamie Johnson had more familiarly named him. His deep brown coat shone in the sunlight, and he had excellent confirmation, a perfectly proportioned body that moved with power and agility. He had a dish face, and one of her favorite markings, a stripe that ran down his nose, just left of center.

She shielded her eyes with her hand and observed with some amusement Jamie's attempts to acquaint Wyly with Harvey's idiosyncracies. Wyly was being his typically cocky self. She could read his body language from half across the paddock: he didn't need anyone, least of all some kid from California young enough to be his son, to tell him how to ride a horse.

He approached a jump, then circled out at the last minute.

"Good decision. That's what I saw. You were right on the half stride. Come back around, and let him come forward a little more," Jamie suggested.

Grace walked out to the middle of the course, just behind Jamie. Wyly approached the jump again and once again circled out.

"It was right there," Jamie said, barely masking his frustration. "Just come back and jump the jump. He'll see the distance if you can't. Just support him with your leg."

The horse had great animation, terrific power behind his stride, which increased markedly as he moved toward the jump. But Wyly pulled him up short and stopped three or four strides before the fence. Provoked by the younger man's suggestions, he demanded, "Son, why don't you just pipe down and let me get the feel of him?"

"He knows what he's doing," Jamie shot back. Lowering his voice, he muttered, ". . . more than you do, you belligerent son of a bitch."

Wyly grimaced at Jamie from his perch almost six feet off the ground. "Son, I've been doin' this since you were in short pants," he reminded him.

"Thank God I'm not your son, you hardheaded bastard. You don't know your ass from Bakersfield," Jamie said under his breath.

Wyly glanced over and suddenly took notice of Grace. "Hey there!" he greeted her.

"Oops!" Jamie's cheeks flushed with embarrassment as he realized she must have overheard his remarks about her father.

Grace grinned. "I feel for you, buddy."

Wyly dismounted the horse. "Take him around a few times!" he said, thrusting the reins at Grace. "Get on up there."

She vaulted onto the horse and tightened the stirrup on her right side.

"There?" asked Jamie, tightening the one on her left. She smiled down at him and realized that she'd chosen the more difficult method of springing up and into the saddle instead of the normal mount because she'd wanted to show off for him. Now, it was her cheeks that flamed bright red as they stared at each other.

"That's good. He's big," she said and led Harvey onto the course.

"You want to see a girl who can ride . . . !" Wyly said proudly.

"Oh, I remember." Jamie followed her with his gaze. "She was hell on wheels. Why'd she quit?"

"Who the hell knows? She's still as good as she ever was."

Grace took a minute or two to get a sense of Harvey. All horses had their own distinctive character and quirks, just as people did. Some hated being bathed; others loved nothing more than a good dunk in the pond. Some were stubborn and resisted the jumps; others relished the work and loved the competition.

"Hey, now, Harvey. You're a good boy," she murmured, patting his neck as she lined up for the first jump.

"Shorten your reins! Take a feel of his mouth," Wyly called out to her.

She ignored him and easily cleared the jump. She didn't need his directions. Riding was like breathing, something she did instinctively, without having to give it any thought. Except when Wyly critiqued her technique, which he'd done from the first day she had climbed on a horse.

"Back it up with your leg, girl!" he yelled as she approached the next jump.

Harvey was paying close attention to her signals. Though he seemed to lack a certain level of confidence, he had a generous stride and a lot of heart. He had been well trained, but needed more seasoning to overcome his timidity. He was a good investment, she decided, even if he was still a bit green.

Jamie smiled his approval when she trotted past him. "You're good. You're right on it," he said.

They flew over the third jump.

"Push him now!" shouted Wyly.

Grace felt herself tensing up. Why couldn't he keep his mouth shut and just let her be? She knew what she was doing. Any fool could see that . . . except for Wyly.

She cleared the next one. Harvey was lengthening his stride now, approaching the jumps more aggressively.

"That's it," Jamie yelled. "You're perfect!"

As if in counterpoint, Wyly immediately followed up with, "Balance him! Get him off his forehand."

Jamie studied Wyly, wondering why he persisted in correcting Grace even though she was so obviously doing everything exactly right. Her resentment of Wyly's criticisms showed in the grim set of her lips as she approached an oxer, a wide jump with a spread of almost five feet.

"Ride into the base!" he instructed her.

Damnit! She didn't need him to tell her what do do. She pulled Harvey off the course, trotted back around to Wyly, and jumped off. "Here, Daddy, you ride the goddamned horse!" she said and tossed him the reins.

Some things never changed. He'd used that same voice all through her childhood, always correcting her, never once allowing her the freedom to ride for pure pleasure without passing judgment on her performance.

"When'd you get so sensitive?" he asked, clearly startled by her reaction.

"Well, that answers that," Jamie said to himself as Grace stalked off without another word to either one of them.

~

The rest of the weekend passed without any blowups between Grace and Eddie, Grace and Wyly, Emma Rae and Eddie. Caroline spent most of Sunday afternoon with her father, and Grace made sure not to be home when he returned her to Emma Rae's just after supper.

The more time they spent apart, the more bewildered she was. She felt as if she were wandering through an emotional labyrinth of tortuous, dead-end paths, with no idea how to extricate herself. What was it she wanted from him: an apology? an explanation? a solemn vow never to look at another woman again for as long as he lived? a reconciliation? a divorce?

She missed him terribly. She ached for him in bed. She could hardly sleep for wondering whether he was consoling himself in the arms of Miss Red Crepe Suit. Exhausted from the strain of trying to maintain a cheerful appearance, she was starting to fray at the edges by the time she joined her parents for lunch on Monday.

Despite the elegance of Georgia and Wyly's home, with its handpainted wallpaper, Aubusson rugs, and one-of-a-kind antique pieces, the Kings were down-to-earth folks who ran a working farm. Georgia considered it her duty and privilege to provide a hearty meal every day at noon sharp for her family and whoever else cared to join them. Biscuits, fried chicken, green beans, stewed tomatoes, and corn pudding were the standard fare. The portions were huge, enough to feed an army. Georgia was famous for her hospitality; everyone from the trainers and stable hands to neighbors and visiting horsebreeders knew that there was always a place to sit and more than enough to eat at the Kings' long dining room table.

Occasionally, as today, no guests appeared at the door, and the family dined alone. Grace and Emma Rae had just finished helping Georgia and Eula put out the food when Wyly showed up and took his place at the head of the table.

"Hello, Mother," he said as the others took their seats.

They bowed their heads for a moment of silent grace. Then Wyly said, "Amen," and the bowls and platters were quickly passed around.

Grace had avoided her parents for most of Saturday afternoon and Sunday, because she was determined not to talk to either one of them about Eddie until she was clearer about her own feelings. She had almost decided to drive into town rather than join them for lunch and was therefore relieved when Georgia turned to her and asked, "Grace, will you look at the catering thing with me later?"

"Sure," she said, hoping that Georgia would stick to the topic of what to serve at the Grand Prix party and not get started again about Eddie. "Can you pick up Caroline while I go to Charity League?"

Georgia nodded. "Yes, but I've got the museum board at five-thirty."

Wyly chuckled and reached for another helping of fried chicken. As if Georgia weren't sitting just across the table from him, he said to no one in particular, "If she thinks I'm buying shrimp for five hundred people, she's got another think coming."

"Well, we'll see," Georgia said with a smile that told her daughters the decision had already been made.

"Where's Caroline?" Wyly asked.

Grace finished spreading butter on a biscuit. "At school." Since this was a school day, there was no reason why he shouldn't know exactly where Caroline was. She took a bite of the biscuit and waited for the inevitable follow-up to his question.

Wyly didn't disappoint her. "I guess she must be missing her daddy pretty good by now," he said.

What little appetite she'd had instantly vanished. "Yes, I'm sure she is," she replied, carefully laying her silverware across her plate.

He poured himself another glass of ice tea, then said, "You're aware that we're involved in a real estate deal with Eddie and his dad. Emma Rae mention anything about that to you at all?"

"Yes, Daddy, I'm aware of it. The Wheeler Farm Project. I'm very aware of it."

"So then, you know how uncomfortable it makes all of us for you and Eddie to be having these kinds of problems in the middle of what could be a very lucrative situation for everyone."

"Yes," she said, glancing across the table at Emma Rae in a silent plea for help.

"I talked to Eddie again last night. He wants to make amends. He's willing to do whatever it takes to work this thing out."

"The marriage or the deal?" she asked, furious that he and Wyly had gone behind her back to barter over the future of her marriage like a couple of horse thieves.

"Don't you get smart with me," he warned.

95

"It's a legitimate question," Emma Rae chimed in.

Wyly waved his fork at her. "I'm talking to your sister."

"I know" she said agreeably. "I'm just following along in the conversation for the hell of it."

Wyly glared at her, seemed to decide it wasn't worth his while to tangle with her, then quickly resumed his dialogue with Grace. "Under the circumstances, don't you think it would be in everybody's best interest, but especially Caroline's, for you and Eddie to sit down and talk?" he said in a tone that was meant to imply he was the world's most reasonable human being.

Eula walked into the room, sensed the hostility in the air, and quickly retreated to the kitchen.

"I guess that depends on who you mean by everybody," said Grace.

She saw Georgia gently shake her head at Wyly, as if to remind him to watch his tongue. She wondered whether her mother had known beforehand that Wyly was planning to talk to Eddie, or whether that was something Wyly had undertaken purely on his own initiative. She guessed the latter, though she suspected Georgia agreed that the marriage should be salvaged, if only for Caroline's sake. She knew how Georgia felt about divorce: it was the coward's choice, arrived at by *other* people's children, but never by her daughters. Certainly not by Grace, whom she trusted always to behave in a manner that reflected well on the family.

"Now, listen, honey," Wyly went on, speaking in the same tone she'd heard him use when he was trying to strike a bargain with an unwilling customer. "I'm not sayin' that he hasn't done anything wrong. He knows he has. But he's a good father and a good provider, and that's not so easy to come by. And he has a lot of other fine qualities—"

"Then you marry him!" she cut in, fed up with her parents' commercials on behalf of Eddie Bichon.

His patience worn thin, Wyly pounded his fist on the table. "Now, listen, child!" he declared. "People have survived a lot worse tragedies than this. You are a grown woman, and you are too old to come runnin' home! You can't work things out, that's one thing, but you haven't even tried! And that I won't have! Do you understand what I'm saying?"

For years, she had disciplined herself to accommodate his pronouncements, tolerate his opinions, work around his interference. Now, he was so far off base that she couldn't bear to listen to another word.

"I think so, Daddy," she said, quietly at first. "What you're telling me is that if I'd just eat shit, politely with a knife and fork—"

"Oh, Grace, please!" Georgia objected.

"—and just learn to swallow handfuls of what-

97

ever kind of bullshit he wants to serve up to me, then everything will just be A-okay!" Grace shouted, ignoring her mother's tsks of disapproval. "That's it, right? That's basically what you're saying, isn't it, Daddy? Isn't it?"

She slammed her hand on the table and hit the side of her plate, spilling the contents of her plate all over herself. She stared mournfully at the string beans and stewed tomatoes strewn across the lap of her skirt, then jumped up and stormed out of the room.

"Nice going, Daddy. You handled that like a pro," Emma Rae said.

"You . . . better watch out!" Wyly yelled. "I have just about had it with you!"

Emma Rae shook her head disapprovingly. "How you could talk to her like that with what she's going through! It just makes me sick," she declared to Wyly. Then she glared at her mother. "And why can't you ever make him shut up when you know he's going to say something stupid?"

She stood up, threw her napkin onto the table, and left her parents to sort things out between the two of them.

Georgia leaned back in her chair and stared at her husband. She agreed with him, of course. Grace owed it to herself at least to *listen* to Eddie. There was no such thing as a perfect husband; Georgia knew that as well as the next woman. The secret of a good marriage was a wife's ability to close her eyes to her husband's foibles and failings. She had thought that Grace had learned that by now, but apparently not. Did that mean she had failed her as a mother and a role model?

Sometimes life was just too complicated. She had no doubt that eventually things would right themselves and that they would all go back to normal. But in the meantime, there was all this shouting and unpleasantness and difficult talk at the table.

She sighed as she contemplated her husband, who was looking distinctly unrepentant. They had been married thirty-eight years, and there was still so much about him she didn't begin to fathom. What *could* have been going through his mind when he had talked to Grace like that? Didn't he understand anything about his daughters?

"Wyly, why did you do that?" she asked quietly.

He scowled and pushed away his plate. His lunch was ruined. "All our friends complain about how their kids grow up and go off and they never hear from them anymore," he said bitterly. "Why in the hell can't that happen to us?"

～

Emma Rae came charging into her house with a head full of steam she had worked up over Wyly's bungling attempt to play the peacemaker. She found Grace on her knees in the guest room, items

99

of clothing strewn about the floor. "Are you all right?" she asked.

"Yes!" Grace said, rooting through her suitcase for a clean pair of riding pants. "Yes! I'm just . . ." She threw up her hands in disgust and sat back on her heels. "What did I do? I was going to be a goddamn large animal vet. I only had a year to go . . . and look at me. How did this happen?"

"Oh, so you were just standing there?"

Grace was expecting sympathy and sisterly support. She wasn't prepared for Emma Rae's look of incredulity. "What do you mean?" she said, taken aback by the flash of anger in her eyes.

"How did this *happen* to you?" Emma Rae marched over to the bookshelf on the far wall and grabbed one of the photo albums. She furiously flipped through it, found what she had been searching for, and dropped the open album onto Grace's lap. She pointed to a picture of Grace and Eddie, both completely wrecked, their arms around each other, their heads thrown back in unrestrained hysterical laughter.

"What's that?" she demanded.

Grace stared at the picture. She hadn't seen it in years. The two of them looked so young and carefree. So much in love. Or were they just drunk? "It's the Chi O Sadie Hawkins dance," she said slowly, still puzzled by Emma Rae's anger.

"That's right! Exhibit A! Sadie Hawkins! *You*

asked him!" Emma Rae stabbed at the picture with her finger.

"So? What's your point?"

"My point is that none of this just happened to you! Let's face it, Grace, you were not just hit by a truck!" yelled Emma Rae.

"I never said that!" Grace defended herself. "Besides, who left, huh? Who left who?" She gave up on finding the clean jodhpurs, pulled on a pair that were definitely in need of a washing, and tossed her skirt on top of the jumbled pile of clothes in the suitcase.

"Did you really leave, or are you just waiting for him to suffer enough?" Emma Rae challenged her.

"I have to go," she said curtly. "I have a Charity League meeting."

She had pulled the same damn trick ever since they were kids, running off whenever the conversation didn't go to her liking, or got too hot for her to handle. She would get Emma Rae all stirred up and primed for a fight, then . . . boom! In a split second, she'd be gone, rushing off to a lesson or a meeting or a date, while Emma Rae was left behind, sputtering with rage.

Grace had always managed to get the last word, but not this time. Emma Rae refused to sit back and let her play the martyr.

"Another perfect case in point!" she said.

"Emma Rae! Contrary to whatever Daddy may say, I *am* facing up to my responsibilities," said

Grace, ticking them off on her fingers. "I have a cookbook to put out, a daughter to raise, and the goddamn Winter Grand Prix, and I just don't have time for the nervous breakdown that I deserve! So don't ask me to stop and think!"

Even now, when it counted most, Grace was more inclined to run away from the truth than confront it. No time to stop and think? That was precisely what she most needed to do. How else was she going to figure out where to go next with Eddie? Did she think the answer would come to her in a dream, that she'd wake up the next morning, fully enlightened about whether or not to try and save her marriage?

"No, you're right, Grace. Let's just wait and see what happens," she said and headed for the door.

"I only asked him because he was a good dancer," Grace called after her.

The front door banged shut. Emma Rae was gone.

She glanced again at the photo album and thought back to the Chi O Sadie Hawkins party. Asking Eddie had taken every bit of courage she had, and then some. She'd almost fainted when he'd accepted her invitation.

The chemistry between them was obvious in the pictures. They'd danced all night, every slow dance and just about every one of the fast ones, as well. They couldn't keep their eyes or hands off each other. How long had it been since she'd felt that same thrill of excitement when he walked into the room? When had they stopped holding hands, stopped groping for each other in the darkness?

She flipped the pages until she came to a shot of Eddie staring full-face into the camera. She had taken the picture about a month before their wedding, in front of her sorority house. Eddie and a bunch of his friends had dropped by for a game of touch football with her sorority sisters. They had played for a couple of hours, tearing all over the lawn and drinking beer and screaming with laughter. Eddie was flashing his killer smile. She smiled now, too, remembering that perfect, magnolia-scented spring day when she had felt sorry for anyone who wasn't as much in love as she was.

A sob caught in her throat. She slammed the album shut. That irresistible smile—and her own naiveté—had landed her in this mess. She stuffed her clothes back into the suitcase. It was time to go talk recipes with the ladies of the Charity League.

～

"Grace! Wait!"

Grace turned, peered over the top of her cookbook files, and saw Lorene frantically waving at her from the other end of the Charity League hallway. Lorene's high heels clicked loudly against the tile floor as she hurried to catch up with Grace. Her normally placid face was creased in a worried frown.

"I've been trying to call you," she said, pulling Grace into one of the rooms off the main corridor.

"What's wrong?" asked Grace.

Lorene nervously patted her flowered skirt. "I heard . . . that you left Eddie," she whispered.

So it was already common knowledge. She should have guessed that it wouldn't take long for people to start talking about them. She just wished she knew herself whether she and Eddie were through before the gossip mongers made the decision for them. She shrugged. "Well, Lorene, you know—"

"Grace," said Lorene. She bit her lip nervously. "You would tell me if it had anything to do with me, wouldn't you?"

Grace stared at her, puzzled by the question. "Of course, I . . ."

Her voice trailed off as the implications sunk in. She wanted to hurl the cookbook files onto the floor and run as far away as possible from Lorene's horrible revelation. That son of a bitch lowlife! Silly little Lorene Rhiner, of all people! Eddie had always made fun of Lorene, with her simpering smile and sly comments. But when? And for how long?

"—would, Lorene, but after all, that was . . . God, how long ago was that?" she prompted her.

"Oh, God, it was just before I was pregnant with Annie. So let's see . . ."

Grace's eyes widened. Annie? Eddie's daughter? Was it possible?

"Oh, no!" Lorene quickly reassured her. "Not *just* before! No. God, no! Poor child, she got Tuffy's looks and my brain. But before that. You know how Tuffy was always so competitive with Eddie. We were having a time, I mean, Tuffy just wouldn't stay put, and you know how nothing makes a man pay attention like a little competition. But I mean, that's all it was. It was nothing."

She touched Grace's arm, a gesture of sisterhood.

Grace shook her head. What was she supposed to say in response to Lorene's remarkable admission? She looked down at Lorene's hand on her arm. A huge diamond ring winked at her. Had that been Tuffy's way of narrowing the competition between himself and Eddie?

Lorene seemed relieved finally to have unburdened herself of her troubling secret. She patted her hair, shifted her bag from one shoulder to the other, and eagerly awaited Grace's absolution.

"That guy has such . . . heart. I'm so happy he could be of use to you. He's so generous that way."

Lorene smiled, misinterpreting Grace's sarcasm for forgiveness. "I know you and Eddie will work it out. Underneath, he's a really good guy," she said warmly as she moved off in the direction of their meeting.

Grace sleepwalked after her, as shocked as if

Lorene had hauled off and whacked her over the head with a two-by-four. The truth—in its barest, starkest form—was a terrifying beast from whose grip she could not escape. She felt irrevocably changed by Lorene's confession, forced to look at her world with an entirely new lens. She had always accepted Georgia's belief that people were essentially good and trustworthy. But if so-called friends like Lorene could betray her so casually, how was she ever again supposed to trust anyone?

She looked around at the other Charity League members and wondered what they knew that they weren't telling her. Suddenly, she realized that when it came to keeping secrets, she was as guilty as the rest of them.

Norma's voice gradually penetrated the fog in her brain. "Okay, at this time, I open the floor to any new business," she said, banging her president's gavel. "Any new business?"

As if she were observing the meeting from a place on the ceiling, Grace noticed several hands being raised.

Norma called first on Mary Jane Parker.

"Anybody who wants to volunteer for the Christmas bazaar should sign up with me or call me by the end of next week. That's all," said Mary Jane.

"Anybody else?" asked Norma. "Lucy?"

"If everybody would please make a commitment to sell at least ten raffle tickets, that would be great," said Lucy. "If you don't think you can, we need to know, so call me or Edna."

The fog in Grace's brain had begun to recede. She had some new business she wanted to discuss. She raised her hand.

"Grace?" said Norma.

Grace stood up. "Yes," she said, hugging her files against her chest, "I was just wondering, who else here has fucked my husband?"

There was a loud, communal gasp. A hush fell in the room. One of the women cleared her throat nervously.

"Lorene was just telling me how he'd been kind enough to help her out by sleeping with her to make Tuffy straighten up," Grace went on. "I was just wondering if, you know, this is a regular service he provides to all my friends, or what."

Someone in the back row tittered. The women gazed up at Grace, their eyes wide, curious, expectant. They were enjoying this, she realized suddenly. The same way they enjoyed reading romance novels or watching soap operas. It was a great story—full of drama and passion and intrigue. Best of all, it was happening to *someone else*. Well, they were wrong about that. It was happening to *all* of them. But they were turning a blind eye, ignoring the unmistakeable signs just as stubbornly as she had.

"Grace," Norma broke in nervously, "this isn't the appropriate time—"

"I know that, Norma!" she snapped. "It's probably not the appropriate time to tell you that your husband keeps half the hookers in town in high heels either! But I'm asking anyway, if there is anyone else here who for any reason has had any kind of sex with my goddamn husband! I think I have the right to know!"

An unfamiliar voice—hoarse and raucous— echoed in her ears. She caught her breath and realized that it was her voice she was hearing. She sounded like a preacher at a revival meeting, exhorting his congregants to repent or be damned.

"Grace . . ." Lucy appealed to her gently, "you're losing it."

She hated to argue with her best friend, but Lucy was wrong. She had lost it that first moment she had seen Eddie kiss Miss Red Crepe Suit. Now, she was about to embark on the process of regaining her sanity.

"Okay. I'll tell you what," she announced to the women, who sat unmoving and attentive to her every word. "I'll start. Mary Jane, remember that redheaded waitress at the country club? About twenty-two, built? She and Calhoun . . . well, let's just say they were more than friends. And Kitty, did you know that Bill had an affair with Dr. Davenport's dental hygienist?"

She smiled at the two women she had just named, welcoming them into the club which she had only recently joined herself. Not a very exclusive club, but it *was* coed, and all ages were welcome.

Mary Jane burst into tears. Kitty swayed in her chair and looked as if she might faint. Two of her close friends, seated on either side, reached over to steady her. Mary Jane yelled something at Grace, but the other women in the room were talking too loudly for Grace to make out what she had said.

"And, Eleanor, you slept with George McMurray in Antigua. Lucy told me," Grace shouted to be heard above the growing din in the room.

Lucy, horrified by Grace's tale-telling, leaped to her feet. "Okay, Grace! That's enough!" she cried.

She shook her head. She had seen the light and wanted to share it with everyone. "Lucy, why shouldn't we be honest? You're supposed to be my *friends*! And if your friends won't tell you the truth, who will?"

Her question hit its mark like a well-aimed arrow. The room fell silent again.

"I mean," she said, posing the even more important question, "who are we trying to kid?"

A hand waved timidly in the air. Anne Moncure, a shy, pretty woman who rarely spoke up at the meetings, raised her voice and appealed to Grace for clarification.

"Does just making out count?"

5
~

The Charity League meeting had ended early and abruptly. It took a near riot for Grace to finally stop talking. Norma's vigorous use of her gavel went unheeded as the women sought solace from one another, and neighbors turned on neighbors, demanding confirmation of long-held suspicions. In the midst of all the pandemonium, Grace stood at the front of the room, gravely nodding her head, past caring that many of the women were turning their anger at their husbands and friends against her.

Her whole life she had minded her manners and smiled and pretended to be fine even when she had been angry or sad. She was flooded with relief now from finally having obeyed her instinct instead of her upbringing. There would be repercussions, of course. You couldn't light a stick of dynamite and not expect an explosion to follow. She would have to make some apologies, patch things up with Lucy, prepare to be disliked for a while.

None of that mattered at the moment. She felt a lightness in her bones that gave her the strength to leave the cookbook files in a neat little pile on top of Norma's podium and hold her head erect as she walked out of the building into the fresh winter air.

Her elation continued into the evening, when she actually found herself humming as she caught up with work in her office. When the telephone rang, she reached for it without thinking. Her good mood lasted for as long as it took to say, "Hello," and get Eddie's response at the other end.

"What are you doing?" he yelled.

That damn grapevine! The phone lines must have been buzzing. She wondered how many different versions of her outburst he had been treated to. She swung her legs up onto the desk, turned on the speakerphone, and prepared herself for verbal combat.

"I mean, Jesus Christ, Grace!" he shouted. "You probably just busted up about everybody's marriage we know!"

What a hypocrite he was. "Well, I'm sure you can help 'em out," she said nastily. "You're such a goddamn Good Samaritan."

"Come on, Grace," he said, softening his tone. "We can't do this. Let's get some help or something! George and Trudy, they went through something like this, and they worked it out."

Maybe that's how George told the story, but she knew better. "Trudy's on Prozac, Eddie," she informed him.

"Well, don't we know any normal people we can talk to?" He was pleading again, his voice dripping honey like a hive in the full heat of summer.

She knew that voice so well. But this time she wasn't about to be seduced by his sweetness and charm. "No one springs to mind," she said.

"All right, Grace!" He suddenly reverted to his earlier, furious self. "What? Do you want a divorce? What do you want? I'll do whatever you say!"

"A divorce?" She sat up and moved closer to the phone, as if needing that proximity to decide how seriously to take him. She had considered divorce, but only in the privacy of her own mind. Hearing him offer it as a possibility was unexpected and frightening.

"Is that what you want?" he asked.

She turned the question back on him, trying not to betray her anxiety. "Is that what *you* want?"

She wasn't the only person in the barn waiting for his answer. Just a few feet away, perched on a step outside one of the stalls, Caroline held her breath and tried not to cry.

She hadn't planned to eavesdrop on her parents' conversation. She had sneaked over to the barn to say good night to the horses. When she heard the phone ring, and her father's voice came drifting over the ceilingless space above the office, she had almost run next door to talk to him. But then all the screaming and shouting had begun, and she had been too scared to do anything but cross her fingers and pray that they would make up.

"I said I think we ought to talk!" Eddie reminded Grace. "If you don't want to do that, then I don't know what else to do! Am I supposed to just call you up and let you tell me what a piece of shit I am for the rest of my sorry-ass life?"

"I don't know," she said.

She picked up a pen, scribbled the word "divorce" on her notepad, then scored it with heavy, dark lines until she tore through the paper. It hit her then that what she really wanted was for Eddie somehow to make it all better between them. She wanted him to fold her in his arms and console her, the way he calmed and comforted Caroline when she woke up screaming in the night when she was having a bad dream.

"Are you asking me to decide right this minute? Aren't you jumping the gun a little here?"

She bit her lip, immediately regretting the harshness of her tone. *Sorry,* she mouthed in the direction of the speakerphone, but she couldn't bring herself to say the word aloud.

"Hey, you're calling the shots, Grace," said Eddie. "I'm the asshole, right? I mean, if you're too goddamned busy, God forbid anything as insignificant as our marriage comes between you and a goddamn horse show!"

Before she had a chance to tell him that the damn horse show had nothing to do with anything, there was a sharp click, then a dial tone. Her temples throbbed with pain as she punched the button that turned off the speakerphone. The dial tone stopped, but her headache was getting worse by the moment.

Was this how marriages ended, in a barrage of angry words, insults, and misunderstandings? Now what? Where were they supposed to go from here? She leaned her head on her palms and felt the cold, smooth surface of her wedding band press against her eyebrow. Eddie's ring—the same design in a much larger width—was tucked away in one of his drawers. She wore hers all the time, even when she washed dishes or went swimming.

She slid it off now and studied her left hand. Her naked ring finger was marked by a slight indentation, paler than the rest of her skin. She cradled the ring in her hand and marveled that something so light could make such a strong impression. Then she clenched her fist around it, closed her eyes, and searched the darkness for answers that refused to come.

On the other side of the plywood wall that separated Grace's office from the rest of the barn, Caroline looked up and saw Jamie silently beckoning her to come with him. She felt so sad that it helped to slip her hand into his and let him lead her toward the other end of the barn.

They were halfway to the door when she stopped, too tired to walk another step. She wished her daddy were there to carry her back to the house. She was too shy to ask Jamie for a piggyback ride, but he seemed to know what she wanted. He also seemed to know, as he picked her up in his arms, that they had to be very quiet. She had heard from her mother's voice how angry she was with her father, and she didn't want to upset her mother any more than she already was. Something had to be done to make them love each other again. Wrapping her arms around Jamie's neck, she gazed up at the starry sky and made a silent wish: *please, God, don't let my parents get divorced.*

~

When Grace got back to the house, Emma Rae was snuggling on the couch with Hoover, watching an old Barbara Stanwyck movie. Despite her fatigue, Grace felt too keyed up to sleep, so she went into the kitchen and made a big bowl of popcorn, then joined her sister in front of the TV set. But after just a few minutes, her mind drifted to Eddie, and soon she was so lost in thought she didn't even notice Emma Rae spraying her with popcorn to get her attention.

A loud knock at the door jolted her out of her

trance. She sat bolt upright and threw Emma Rae a questioning look. They had the same thought: Eddie? At this hour?

"Hoover! No! Quiet!" Emma Rae shushed the dog, who was barking wildly, as if in protest against this unexpected intrusion upon his otherwise peaceful evening.

She went to the window, peered out into the night, and was surprised by who she found standing on her porch. "It's Jamie," she told Grace.

Grace was hardly in the mood for company, but it would be too rude to turn him away.

"Hey, Jamie," said Emma Rae, opening the door for him.

He smiled, and she found herself wondering what he looked like beneath his jeans and T-shirt. "Grace here?" he asked.

Ah, well, he wasn't her type, anyway.

"Oh, hey," he said to Grace. "Can I talk to you for a second?"

Grace didn't believe him at first. Caroline had to be in bed. She had tucked her in hours ago. But after a quick check of the guestroom, she threw on a sweater and hurriedly walked Jamie across the yard to the barn.

As they slipped through the partly open door, Jamie gestured for her to follow him to Possum's stall. Sure enough, her daughter was stretched out on the hay-strewn floor, her riding boots visible beneath the horse blanket in which she had wrapped herself. Her eyes were tightly shut, and she lay very still, as if she were fast asleep. But Grace knew from her quivering eyelids that she was only pretending.

"Caroline." She knelt by her side and touched her shoulder. "C'mon. We're got to go."

There was a long pause, then, "No. I'm asleep."

"Come on, honey. You can't sleep here," Grace whispered, stroking her daughter's cheek.

Caroline opened her eyes and shook her head. "Yes! No!" She blurted out her confusion. "I don't want to sleep there."

Grace gently nudged her up off the floor. "Why not?"

"It's hot," Caroline said, pouting.

"We'll take the covers off. Come on." She pulled at the blanket and tried to pick her up.

But Caroline fought her. She crossed her legs and arms, hunkered down, and said, "It stinks."

Grace tried to remind herself that Caroline was just a child, who must be feeling as if her world was being turned upside down. But she was tired, and her patience was wearing thin. "It does not stink! Now, come on," she urged her daughter.

Caroline refused to budge. There was no point trying to reason with her. Grace grabbed her around the waist and managed to heave her up into her arms. Jamie trailed behind them as she carried Caroline through the breezeway, back toward the house.

Motherhood, she thought. She had undertaken the job so lightly, for the simple reason that she had always wanted to have children. Not once during the pregnancy had she spent even a single moment reflecting on what it meant to be a parent.

Perhaps parenthood was something you couldn't understand until you actually held the baby in your arms and realized that from now on, everything you did—every choice or decision you made—affected this child. You could stop being someone's wife or lover or friend. But you could never stop being a mother.

Caroline was getting almost too heavy to carry. One minute she could act so grown up, the next second she was just a little kid again, who slept with her teddy bear and her dolls and the picture of Possum under her pillow. No wonder she had gone to sleep in his stall. It had to feel a lot safer there than in Emma Rae's guest room.

She would talk to her tomorrow. She would explain that Mommy and Daddy were having an argument, but that they both still loved her very much. She would tell her not to worry, somehow reassure her that everything would be all right.

They had almost reached the house. She buried her nose in Caroline's hair and inhaled her lovely, sweet smell.

Caroline sighed contentedly. Then she raised her head and turned her sleepy eyes on Grace. "Mom?" she asked. "Are you gonna get a divorce?"

Caroline fell asleep almost as soon as Grace tucked her into bed. Grace lay next to her for a long time afterward, wanting to be there just in case she woke up again. A sliver of moonlight fell through the window, which she had opened at Caroline's insistence. In the dark, she could just make out her daughter's features.

She would never willingly do anything to hurt this beautiful, precious child—and yet, Caroline *was* suffering. It didn't matter whether it was her fault or Eddie's, or who was to blame. Drawing that distinction missed the point, which was that their pain was secondary to their daughter's.

Resolving that she would somehow make it up to Caroline, she very carefully slid out of bed and closed the window. Then she pulled the covers up to Caroline's chin and tiptoed into the living room. No one was there, but she could hear Emma Rae and Jamie talking softly on the porch.

"Is she okay?" asked Jamie as she stepped outside.

She sat down next to him on the steps and sighed. "Yes. God, thank you so much. I didn't even know she was out."

Emma Rae yawned loudly and stood up. "Okay. I'm going to bed. I'll see you tomorrow."

She went inside, and a few seconds of companionable silence passed. An owl hooted near the barn and was answered by a horse's neighing. A light flickered off at her parents' house.

"She comes down every night," said Jamie. "Visits Possum."

• Grace propped her elbows on her knees and leaned forward to stare at the stars. "God, she's worse than I was."

Jamie chuckled. "She's a great kid," he said. "Smarter than a treeful of owls." He hesitated for a scant moment, then said gently, "I wouldn't talk on that speakerphone anymore, though."

"Jesus Christ!" Caroline had been in the barn the whole time she was talking to Eddie. And probably Jamie had heard a good part of it, as well. She was mortified, and furious at herself for being so stupid. "I'm unfit," she said, wondering what he must think of her.

"No, you're not. Going through this shit makes you crazy," he said.

He stretched out his legs and shifted his weight to get more comfortable, and she suddenly became aware of his well-muscled arm only an inch or two away from hers.

"How long were you together?" she asked, turning her head slightly to get a better view of his face, which was bathed in the pale yellow light of a Chinese lantern left over from one of Emma Rae's parties.

"Ten years," he said flatly.

"Me, too. What happened?"

"It's a long, goddamned story." He exhaled sharply and dug the heels of his boots into the pebbles that bordered the porch. "She met somebody else. She said she didn't love me anymore. Not a whole hell of a lot you can do about that."

Her mother had taught her not to pry into other people's private affairs. But Georgia's rules weren't working very well for her lately, and she needed help from someone who had already explored this alien territory into which she seemed to be venturing further and further.

"Did you find . . . that you lost your ability to think rationally?" she asked, trying to choose her words carefully.

He laughed, giving it a short, harsh sound that sounded more bitter than amused. "I'm here because of a custody battle over a horse. Does that tell you anything?" He shrugged, and his voice softened, as if he'd suddenly remembered how much less experienced she was in this area. "I don't know, I wish I had some advice. Maybe some people come out the other side wiser or . . . I don't know. Next time I think I'd just rather get shot."

"Well." She gazed at his profile, saw his mouth twist into a caustic smile. "Don't sugarcoat it on my account."

He laughed and pretended to be surprised by her comment. "Do I sound bitter? You'd tell me."

"Oh, no, not at all!" She laughed along with him.

They fell silent again. She thought about Eddie, wondered where he was tonight, then wondered what Jamie was thinking.

"You met her," he said as if in answer to her question.

"I did?"

He nodded. "We came to the party here every year. We sat at the same table once with you and your husband. In fact, he danced with her."

She closed her eyes and pictured Jamie at the Grand Prix party. She came up with an image of a woman who had drunk too much champagne and giggled a lot. "Long black hair?"

"Yeah. He's a hell of a dancer."

"Yeah," she agreed, trying to remember whether Eddie and Jamie's wife had disappeared together at any point during the evening.

He grinned at her. Unexpectedly, they were hugging each other. His arms tightened around her, and she briefly leaned her head against his shoulder. After ten years, it felt strange yet nice to be held that way by a man other than Eddie. She wondered what it would feel like to kiss him, and pulled away before she could translate that thought into action.

"Did we dance?" she asked, noticing how his lips curved upward when he smiled.

"No. We didn't."

She was sure that what she heard in his voice was regret.

She must be losing her mind. She felt like she was back in high school, suddenly smitten with a crush on the new boy in town. After they said good night, she went inside and turned off the lights. Then she stood by the window and watched him walk down the road until he disappeared from view.

She knew she shouldn't, but she couldn't stop herself from tiptoeing into Emma Rae's bedroom and whispering, "Are you still up?"

Emma Rae pulled the sheet over her head. "Not technically," she said grumpily.

Grace sat down next to her on the bed and sighed. "God, that guy is so nice."

Emma Rae groaned and gave up trying to sleep. "Yeah, he is." She threw back the sheet and leaned up against the headboard.

"I want to have him over for dinner sometime." Grace giggled and scooted over to lie next to her, the way she used to when they were teenagers. "You think that'd be too weird?"

"Why would it be weird?"

"I don't know. You know."

"You have people over for dinner all the time," Emma Rae reminded her. "You're the world's greatest hostess, for cryin' out loud. What are you gettin' all shy about?"

"I'm not." She shivered, remembering Jamie's arms around her.

Emma Rae grinned wickedly and poked her in the ribs. "Oh, I see. Well, I think you should just give him a call and ask him what he likes to eat. And if he says pussy, tell him to come on over."

Just like in high school! Emma Rae would say anything to shock her. She pulled away from her. "Goddamn, Emma Rae! You are vile!"

Emma Rae turned to face her. "Well, just do something, will you? Do something drastic!"

"Oh, like I haven't already?" Annoyed with her sister for ruining her fun, she announced, "I'm going to bed." But she stopped when she got to the door. "Emma Rae, I know you're disappointed in me," she said, speaking as much to herself as to her sister.

"No." Emma Rae shook her head. "No . . . *for* you, sweetie, not in you."

Grace smiled sadly. Being an adult was so hard. There was too much she didn't know. How was she supposed to teach Caroline all the things a child needed to learn in order to be happy and fall in love with the right person and figure out what she wanted to do with her life?

She had never worried about such questions before. She had just gone along, taking care of Caroline and Eddie, looking after the house, running the stables, doing all the hundreds of little things that added up to being Grace King Bichon.

But was just *going along* enough? Was she cheating Caroline out of some crucial lessons by her example?

"Hey, sleep tight," Emma Rae whispered.

Grace blew her a kiss and went off to dream about being seventeen again, that blessed time before she had realized her actions had consequences, and there were no guarantees things would turn out a certain way just because that's what she wanted.

~

Aunt Rae cut Grace a huge wedge of her coconut cake, laid it on the table next to the cup of coffee she had just poured her, and posed a rhetorical question.

"Will you take some advice from a little ol' lady?"

She didn't bother waiting for Grace's consent before she launched into her recommendation. "You've got to take this bull by the horns, so to speak. Are you gonna see him?"

Grace glanced surreptitiously at her watch. She had stopped by Aunt Rae's house on her way back from town as a favor to Georgia, who wanted to borrow Aunt Rae's antique lace tablecloths. She was already behind schedule and hadn't meant to stay for more than a minute. But Aunt Rae had just taken a cake out of the oven and wouldn't hear of her leaving without joining her for a piece.

The kitchen was warm and sunny and smelled of coconut. Grace could think of a lot worse places to be right then.

"We're supposed to get together to talk tonight," she told Aunt Rae.

Aunt Rae took a bite of cake and smiled with ill-concealed pride in her culinary achievement. "Where?" she asked, watching for Grace's reaction.

"Houston's." Though Grace didn't have much appetite this morning, the fresh baked cake went down easily. She took another forkful and sipped her coffee.

"Oh, no," Aunt Rae declared. "Now, see? He wants to go somewhere where he thinks you won't make a scene, although deep in his heart he knows there is no such place." She shook her head vigorously. "No, you meet him at home. And if I were you . . ."

Her voice trailed off, and her hand stopped midway between the plate and her mouth. She seemed to be lost in deep thought.

Curious now, Grace prompted her. "What?"

"I'd . . ." Her eyes twinkled mischievously.

"What?" Grace repeated herself. Aunt Rae was known to have been a real hell-raiser as a young woman. She was still unpredictable, and fully capable of planning a bit of wickedness now and then.

"I'd make him something special for supper," she said.

Her suggestion was so hopelessly old-fashioned that it made Grace smile. "Aunt Rae, I think it's a little more complicated than that."

Aunt Rae licked the icing off her fork and smiled impishly. "I'm gonna say it again. Make him something special, that he won't forget, ever."

She went over to her cabinet and took out her recipe box. She flipped through the well-thumbed food-stained cards and quickly found what she was looking for.

"Here." She handed Grace a card. "Make him that."

Grace read the recipe aloud. "Broiled salmon with mint mustard sauce. A half-pound salmon fillet, whole grain mustard, quarter cup olive oil, fresh mint leaves, one-eighth teaspoon . . ." She stared at her aunt in stunned amazement, sure that she was misreading the recipe. "Oh my God! But this is . . .".

Aunt Rae chuckled gleefully. "It's not lethal, not in that small dose," she said as calmly as if she were discussing the curative powers of chicken soup. "It will, however, make him sick as the dog that he is. Of course, you have to tell him that you've done it, or it doesn't do any good. I always told Lloyd if he was going to hit me where I lived, then he could expect the same from me. I just think of it as homeopathic aversion therapy."

"Oh, my God!" Grace exclaimed. Whatever her feelings were for Eddie, she hadn't gone so far as to consider poisoning him.

"Sometimes a little near-death experience helps them put things in perspective," Aunt Rae said. She cut two more slivers of coconut cake, poured fresh coffee into her dainty Lenox china cups, and winked at her niece. "Yes, ma'am," she gaily assured her.

~

Georgia's heart ached for Grace, Eddie, and, most of all, for Caroline. She sympathized with Grace's pain. But she was also sure that the sooner Grace and Eddie worked things out and reconciled, the better off everyone would be. Meanwhile, here was Caroline, dragging around as though she had lost her best friend, and neither one of her parents seemed to realize that the poor, dear child was falling apart.

Georgia was utterly at a loss to understand why her sweet, reasonable daughter was being so close-minded and stubborn. It would be another matter altogether if it were Emma Rae, who was just as pigheaded as her daddy. But Grace? What *could* Grace be thinking? How could she live with herself knowing that Eddie was all set to kiss and make up, if only she would let him.

He had behaved very badly; he had admitted that to Wyly. But such things happened in almost every marriage. The shame was how indiscreet he had been, so that poor Grace had had to witness it with her very own eyes. How that must have hurt her! Eddie's mother had spoiled him rotten. But he was such a darling boy . . . who could blame her? Mothers did their very best for their children. Too often those efforts went unappreciated, as Georgia had recently discovered with Grace, who seemed to bristle every time Georgia opened her mouth.

Well, she decided, if she couldn't make any headway with Grace, at least she could give her granddaughter some extra love and attention. Lord knew the child was crying out for help, going off to sleep in Possum's stall. . . .

She had Eula bake Caroline's favorite chocolate pecan pie for dessert. Then, as a special treat, she dug out of the attic their old eight-millimeter home movies that Caroline had been begging to see.

There was no sound, of course, which Caroline found odd after years of watching videos. But the pictures were bright and clear, and the shots of a much younger Wyly in the Grand Prix ring brought tears to Georgia's eyes.

"Who's that Gramps is on there?" Caroline asked.

"That's Pride's Soldier Boy," she said. "This is the year he won Upperville Grand Prix."

Caroline sat transfixed by the image of her grandfather riding into the ring for the awards presentation. He accepted his trophy and medal, then rode past Georgia, who was vigorously applauding him from the stands. She stood up as he passed her and saluted him with her right hand. Wyly touched his finger to the brim of his black hat, then trotted back to the winner's circle to pose for a photograph.

"Why do you always do that when Gramps rides?" asked Caroline.

"Do what?"

"Stand up and give that little wave."

Georgia smiled. "Oh, that's just a thing we do. The first time it just happened. He looked like Prince Charming, and I just stood up," she said, recalling the excitement of that competition. "After that, I don't know. I just always did it."

"Did Gramps ever win Winter National Grand Prix?"

"Not yet," declared Wyly, who had been listening from the doorway.

Startled by his entrance, they jumped off their chairs.

"But I got a good feeling this time." He leaned over Georgia's chair. "I got to go out for a little bit," he said, staring at himself on the screen. "Damn, I was a handsome devil!"

"And so modest!" teased Georgia.

He grinned as he kissed her good night. "Don't you girls stay up too late," he said, blowing a kiss at Caroline.

Caroline blew one back at him. Then she and Georgia turned again to the movie. Now, one of the judges was pinning a ribbon on Wyly's horse's bridle.

Georgia watched as Wyly smiled proudly and took his victory lap around the ring. He certainly had been a handsome devil. Still was. He was right about that. She only hoped he was just as right in predicting his victory this year at the Winter National.

6

~

Grace unwrapped the half pound of salmon she had bought that afternoon and rinsed it under the cold water. She had already mixed most of the other ingredients and thrown them into the food processor. All she had left to do was trim the fish and get rid of the bones, then blend the mint and mustard, and add a dose of Aunt Rae's special, homeopathic sauce.

She felt nervous, not about cooking, which she did with ease and enjoyment, but about seeing Eddie. The realization that they had to come to some sort of resolution about the future scared her. She wasn't ready to concede that their marriage was a complete failure. Nor was she about to welcome him back into her life with wide open arms, as her parents seemed to think she should do. There had to be other alternatives, though she couldn't think what they might be.

She had spent a ridiculous amount of time trying

132

to decide what to wear, changing from pants to skirts to a shirtwaist dress, until finally she had settled on a clean pair of jeans and one of her sexier tops. To remind him what he was giving up, she told herself. She was no kid fresh out of college, like Miss Red Crepe Suit. But she and Eddie had had some pretty passionate moments in bed, before they had both gotten so busy that making love had slipped to the bottom of their priorities list. And, hell, she hadn't even hit thirty yet.

At the precise moment that she picked up her chef's knife, Eddie scared her out of her wits by strolling unannounced into the kitchen. She screamed, and so did he, at the sight of her wielding the long, well-sharpened knife.

Her hand flew to her heart. He was early. She hadn't heard the door open. He could at least have called out her name, given her some warning.

"Hi," she said when her heart stopped pounding.

"Hi." He smiled tentatively, as if he still weren't sure how she was planning to use the knife. He took off his jacket and loosened his tie, a gesture so familiar that for the tiniest second she forgot that tonight's dinner was anything out of the ordinary.

"What are you making?" he asked, coming over to inspect the fish.

She casually covered the recipe with her hand. "Salmon with mint mustard sauce."

"Sounds good," he said.

He sounded different. Eager to please her. Nervous, too. Maybe as nervous as she was.

"Aunt Rae gave me the recipe," she told him, skinning the salmon with one clean, even swipe. "She assures me it's unforgettable."

He helped himself to a slice of tomato from the salad bowl and leaned against the counter, close enough that she could smell his aftershave. His hair was damp, probably because he had just taken a shower. She wondered what he had planned for their dessert.

"Everything you make is unforgettable."

It was his damp hair that got to her. Did he think she was so susceptible to his wiles that all he had to do was pay her compliments and all would be forgiven? "Eddie, please don't start trying to charm me right off the bat like that. That's not what this is about," she said.

"Excuse me. Sorry. I was trying . . ." He shrugged.

She wondered whether she was being too harsh. Maybe he was only trying to make conversation.

"Do you want a drink?" he asked. "I'm gonna get a drink."

A drink was an excellent idea. She nodded yes, and sighed as he left the room. This was too hard. Meeting him at a restaurant might have been a better choice than cooking him dinner as she had done a thousand times before.

He came back into the kitchen with two glasses of bourbon. He added a handful of ice cubes from the freezer and handed her a glass.

"I don't know what we're doing," she said, twirling the ice with her finger.

"Here? Sure, you do." He gulped down a long slug of bourbon. "This is the beginning of my punishment."

Had he somehow gotten wind of Aunt Rae's secret ingredient? She threw him a sideways glance. No, she decided, he was just being difficult. "Don't you start acting all persecuted!" she snapped. "Christ, Eddie, I didn't start this!"

"No, but I'm sure you'll finish it," he shot back and swallowed another long sip of his drink.

His nasty attitude overcame whatever qualms she had had about taking Aunt Rae's advice. "Look! I didn't come here to fight! You said you wanted to get together to talk! So talk!" She turned on the food processor. The machine erupted in a harsh, whirring noise that drowned out Eddie's next few words.

He reached over and turned the processor off. "Cut out this passive-aggressive bullshit, will you?" he shouted.

"I'm not . . ." She struggled to defend herself, and then, suddenly, all the stored-up hurt and fury of the last few days came bursting out of her like a spring flood overflowing the dam. "I wasn't even going to do this! I wasn't even going to get married, for God's sake! I wanted to be a goddamn large animal vet, and date cowboys! Go out with tall, rangy guys that smell like leather and kiss your neck!"

He slammed his glass down on the table. "Well, why the hell didn't you?" he snarled.

"Date cowboys?" She glared at him, daring him to push her further.

"Finish vet school."

"You know why!"

"No, I don't," he said, settling himself into a chair.

He was hateful. She had never imagined that he could be so mean. "Because! I got pregnant! Remember?" she shouted.

"And what?" he jeered. "They closed down all the veterinary schools while you were in labor? I am so sick of having that thrown in my face! Don't blame me! I'm not the reason you failed!"

It took all her self-control not to pick up the salmon fillet and fling it in his face. "Now you're calling me a failure?"

"How many times am I going to have to hear this?" He pursed his lips and raised his voice to imitate her. " 'The only reason I got married is because I got pregnant. I was going to be a vet. I was never even going to get married.' "

"Well, it was true!" She defended herself.

"Then why in God's name did you do it?"

"Why'd you ask me? You're the one who hasn't even stopped dating!"

"Honestly, Grace?" he said. He tilted his chair back, laced his fingers behind his neck, and smiled at her insolently. "I didn't think you'd say yes!"

She was shocked into stillness by his answer. A cold, hard knot lodged itself in her throat, an icy ball of rage that seemed to sprout tentacles and send a chill shooting through her body. She shivered and wrapped her arms around her ribs to warm herself. She turned away from him and stared out the window, finding nothing there except the bleak landscape of their broken marriage.

"Grace . . ." He sounded chastened, as if he knew he had gone too far. "That's not exactly what I meant," he said meekly. "That didn't come out right."

"No." She cleared her throat, trying to form a coherent sentence around the ball of ice. "No, I want to know."

She didn't wait to hear what else he had to say. Quickly, before she gave it too much thought, she picked up the tiny brown bottle that she'd filled with kerosene from the barn and measured the quarter-teaspoon that Aunt Rae's recipe called for. She dumped it into the food processor bowl that held the rest of the green sauce, hesitated briefly, then added another quarter teaspoon. She pressed the "Pulse" bar and let the machine run until the kerosene was completely absorbed in the sauce.

Dinner was almost ready.

She had planned for them to eat in the dining room, but now she changed her mind and decided instead on the kitchen. At the last minute, she stuck a couple of candlesticks in the middle of the table, a halfhearted attempt to create atmosphere. While Eddie tried to keep up a conversation by talking about Caroline, she served the salad first, then the main course.

He seemed not to notice that she wasn't eating the fish, but dug into his portion with the greedy appetite of a starving man. She sipped water and sat silent and despondent as he shoveled in one forkful after another of the salmon.

Finally, he ran out of Caroline anecdotes and got back to the main topic of the evening. "You think this is what I want?" he asked between bites. "Divorced with a kid at thirty-five? Writing alimony checks while you live in the house with some horse guy? Like this is some master plan? I miss . . . I miss . . . I miss Caroline!"

"You should have thought of that!" she said angrily. "Did you think about her? What goes through your mind as you're slipping it in?"

He threw down his fork and scowled. "Well, somebody's got to do it, Grace!"

She gripped the edge of the table to keep from

reaching over and slapping him. "What are you talking about?"

"You never fucking touch me!" he yelled.

"That's not—"

"It's *true*!" he screamed. "Name the last time you initiated anything! It's like that old joke: you know how to paralyze a woman from the waist down? Marry her!"

"Paralyzed! Try *ignored*!" she shouted.

"Bullshit!"

"Don't you start with that 'you're frigid' bullshit," she fumed. "Don't you even say the word! There's nothing wrong with me! I have orgasms every day! It's just easier to do it when you're not in the room!"

He sneered at her. "Same goes double for me."

Enough! She jumped up and grabbed her plate. She flung it into the sink with such force that it shattered as soon as it hit the porcelain. Shards of china and chunks of food flew into the air and spattered everywhere. She gulped back a sob and leaned over the sink, clutching the side as if it were her lifeline to sanity.

Eddie finally broke the silence between them. "All right, Grace. I know I'm a disappointment. What do you want me to do, kill myself?"

"I'm not even blaming you. I stumbled down the primrose path into this trap all by myself," she said wearily.

Some girls would have been upset or scared to

find out they were pregnant without benefit of a wedding band on their left ring finger. She had been thrilled to get the news. She couldn't wait to have a baby. Eddie's baby. They were going to be so happy together, forever and ever, for the rest of their lives. They were going to make lots more babies and stay madly in love and never have any regrets or disappointments.

She had assumed he would propose as soon as she told him the good news, and he hadn't let her down. He had even knelt on one knee to do it, and she had almost fainted from the romance of the moment. Her parents couldn't have been happier. Her mother had wept with joy all through her wedding ceremony, and her father, who had drunk a few too many bourbons, had given a long, rambling toast to Eddie, "exactly the man I would have chosen for my daughter, except she never would have listened to me."

In the midst of all that bliss and excitement about wedding plans and honeymoons and babies, she had totally forgotten about vet school and moving out West to meet cowboys. She had buried that dream so far down it hadn't reemerged until Caroline was in school, and she had gradually remembered what she had really meant to do with her life.

By then, of course, it was too late.

Georgia had raised her on fairy tales about princesses who lived happily ever after. Now, it turned out, she was Rapunzel, trapped in the tower, and she couldn't figure out her escape route.

She couldn't blame Georgia any more than Eddie for luring her into the tower. Georgia had done her best, just as she was doing with Caroline. . . .

Oh, Lord, she was tired. She couldn't ever remember being quite this tired. She wanted to lay her head against the counter and fall asleep. Instead, she turned around and forced herself to concentrate on the words that came spitting out of Eddie's mouth like pellets of hail in a rainstorm.

"Trap? What the fuck do you know about being trapped? You don't want to hear 'frigid'? I don't want to hear 'trapped'! I know what you want from me! You want all this, and for me to come and go quietly without bothering you!"

His face was strangely contorted. His eyes looked red and moist, almost as if he were about to cry.

She shook her head. "That's not what I—"

He cut her off before she could explain what she had meant. "I've done exactly what was expected of me ever since I was a little kid!" he yelled. "School, sports, work, this goddamn Wheeler farm. . . Everything! No! I don't care about horse shows! But there I am, at every goddamn one of 'em! You tell me what's supposed to be in this marriage for me? The woman I married—she liked to dance! She liked to have

141

fun! She liked to fuck! Me! Where is she? Where did she go? I'm all alone here!"

And then he did start to cry . . . heavy, heartwrenching sobs that came from a place deep inside him where he had never been before.

"You don't love me! You don't give a shit about me! It's obvious! You think I don't know if you had it to do over again, you wouldn't choose me? I mean, Grace, did you ever love me? I'm not one of those guys . . . I want to love somebody. You don't even know me. I'm a decent guy . . ."

His shoulders were heaving as he covered his face with his hands and continued to sob uncontrollably. She stood watching him, paralyzed with grief and guilt.

"Eddie." She studied him anxiously. "Eddie, I've done something so wrong. I was trying . . ."

He wiped his eyes on his sleeve. "Forget it, Grace. It doesn't matter—"

"No, no, it does!" She walked across the room to him.

"Oh, God, I don't feel good," he said suddenly.

"Eddie, I think we need to go to the hospital," she whispered.

He gazed up at her with the helpless expression of a wounded animal.

"There's something in the fish," she stammered.

"What? What're you saying?" He shook his head, not understanding.

She leaned over to help him out of his chair. "I was trying to—"

Suddenly, she was covered in vomit.

"Oh my God!" he moaned.

Panic-stricken now, she cried, "Come on! We need . . . I think we should get your stomach pumped!"

"It seems to be pumping itself, Grace!" He doubled over, held his stomach, and puked up another gush of vomit.

"Oh my God! Come on!" she urged, grabbing his arm.

He pitched forward, retching putrid, green liquid that sprayed all over himself, the floor, her arms and legs.

"You bitch! Oh, Jesus! You've killed me!" he groaned.

She was terrified that he might be right. He couldn't seem to stop throwing up the slimy green flow of his partially digested dinner.

She knelt next to him and put her arm around his neck. "Oh my God," she wailed. "What have I done?"

~

Georgia had rarely seen a sorrier sight than her daughter, huddled like a scared child in the far corner of the emergency room waiting area. As she hurried over, Grace dabbed at her shirt, pathetically trying to wipe away the encrusted flecks of dried vomit. Her red-rimmed eyes were puffy from crying, and the tears had left pale white streaks against her even paler cheeks.

"Look at you!" Georgia exclaimed. "Is he all right?"

Grace nodded. Too ashamed to meet her mother's gaze, she hung her head and looked away. In the hour since she had rushed Eddie to the hospital, she had had plenty of time alone to contemplate what a terrible, bad person she was.

"What in the name of God has gotten into you?" Georgia asked reproachfully. "How could you listen to that silly old woman?"

She was afraid she might start to cry again if she tried to talk, so she bit her lip and said nothing. She knew she deserved to be punished, and Georgia's disapproval was about the worst punishment she could imagine. She held her breath, waiting for the inevitable lecture. But Georgia surprised her. Instead of reprimanding her, she took out her handkerchief and applied it to Grace's face, as she used to do when Grace was little.

No lecture, no matter how stern, could have been as humiliating. Grace jerked away from her ministrations, which only made Georgia more resolute to win the tug-of-war with her daughter. Without another word, she yanked her out of the chair, steered her into the bathroom, and turned on the hot water.

"Mother . . ." Grace tearfully protested.

"Don't you 'Mother' me. You are an absolute mess, child." Georgia stuck her handkerchief under the faucet. But before she could begin another assault on Grace, Grace grabbed it away from her.

"That's right, Mother! I'm a mess! Look at me!" she shouted. "I'm an outrage! I'm a disgrace! I'm a failure!"

Georgia had come to the hospital prepared for anything but such histrionic, indulgent displays. "Grace!" she rebuked her. "Don't talk like that! No, you're not!"

"Yes, I am! I drive away and forget my child. I've failed at all of it! Eddie, myself, everything! I've accomplished nothing!" Grace wailed. "Nothing!"

Georgia was aghast that her daughter could get so lost in self-pity and loathing that she seemed to have forgotten the real issues. It was as if some demon had taken over Grace's brain, forcing her to spew out the worst kind of drivel. Georgia simply couldn't listen to another word of it.

"Now you just get a grip on yourself! You think you're the only woman who ever went through something like this? Well, you're not! But there's a little thing called dignity that you'd do well to remember."

"Fuck that, Mother!" Grace retorted.

Georgia inhaled sharply. Why did her daughters *insist* on using such language? "Grace. Stable talk isn't going to make you any stronger."

Which only served to further incite Grace, who by now was all but spitting in her face, "Fuck, fuck, fuck!" She stormed out of the bathroom.

Georgia, for whom behaving like a lady, especially in public, was a moral issue, was right behind her, shouting, "This is not just about you! Do you hear what I'm saying? You have your daughter to think of! Is this what you want her to see? Is it?"

She grabbed Grace's shoulder and gave her a quick, hard shake.

"I'll tell you," she said, keeping a tight grip on Grace. She lowered her voice and made what was for her an extraordinary admission. "I've had my own troubles. It was a long time ago, and I never wanted to saddle you with my problems, but if ever you were to find out, I wanted to be sure you girls would be proud of the way I handled myself."

Grace wrenched herself free and stared at her mother in sheer disbelief. She knew it had to be painful for Georgia even to hint at their family's best-kept open secret. But since she had brought the subject up herself, Grace had the right to correct her absurd misconceptions, particularly if Georgia was so bent on setting herself up as an example to emulate.

"Proud? Are you out of your mind? How the hell were we supposed to be proud that you were oblivious to what was going on right in front of your face?" she hooted.

"What in the name of God are you talking about?" Georgia whispered furiously. "Nothing ever went on 'right in front of my face'!"

"Oh, come on!" Grace scoffed. "Jesus, Mother, you were right there! What about Mrs. Pritchett? Annie Pritchett! Are you going to tell me that you didn't know about that?"

Georgia frowned, appalled by Grace's recklessness. She was willing to admit there'd been certain . . . *problems* in her marriage. But Grace was stepping over a fine line into an area where she didn't belong and about which she knew nothing.

"Annie Pritchett is a friend of ours! Now, Wyly has always been a flirt, and he exudes a certain charm that women find very appealing," she said firmly, hoping Grace would have the good sense to realize there was nothing more about this particular topic she cared to discuss.

Grace rolled her eyes. "Oh, God, Mother!"

"You've let your imagination get the best of you. No. Annie Pritchett is a friend of your father's. That's all!" Georgia insisted.

"Mother, she was only one of many. And don't tell me you didn't know! He was *legendary*, for cryin' out loud," Grace hissed. "And your utter denial does not make me proud! If nothing else, at least Caroline will know that I didn't just lie down like a goddamn doormat and let Eddie walk all over me! How could you think I'd be proud?"

The instant the words were out of her mouth, she saw from Georgia's face that she may as well have stuck a knife in her mother's heart. Georgia's mouth was open in a big, round O, a silent acknowledgment of shock too deep to express aloud. She shook her head from side to side, as if to deny there could be any truth to Grace's statement. Then she pulled her handkerchief out of Grace's hand, shoved it back in her purse, and rushed out of the room.

"Mom, wait!" Grace called.

She hurried after her into the hallway, but she was too late. Georgia had pushed her way onto a crowded elevator, where she stood surrounded on all sides by strangers. The elevator door was already sliding shut, but not before Grace got a glimpse of her, tears splashing down her cheeks.

Grace sagged against the wall and covered her face with her hands. What had she done? First Eddie, now her mother . . . She truly was a monster, poisoning the people she loved with her venomous anger. She took a deep breath, tried to rearrange her face into a semblance of normalcy, and went to check on Eddie.

From the doorway of his room, she couldn't tell whether or not he was awake. His eyes were closed, and his face was totally devoid of color. He was breathing so shallowly that his chest hardly seemed to be moving. But the doctor had assured her that Eddie was not going to die, even if he did have one of the worst cases of food poisoning the doctor had ever treated.

She was about to leave when Eddie's eyes fluttered open. It took some effort, but he raised his arm and beckoned her to his bedside. She tiptoed into the room and managed a weak smile, trying to think how she could ever apologize enough for what she had done. She loved him. She had almost had to kill him to figure that out. She didn't want to divorce him. They had shared too much to give up so lightly on ten years of life together. She had finally decided that no matter what it took, their marriage was worth putting back together.

When she got near enough, he gently pulled her to him and put his lips to her ear. She was about to tell him to save his strength, they could talk later, but he was determined to say something now. His voice was hoarse and low; the doctor had said that his throat would be raw for several days from all that vomiting.

"Get a lawyer," he whispered.

~

Wyly was singing a duet with Tammy Wynette as he flicked on his right blinker. Yessiree, he thought. Life was good. He counted his blessings: a beautiful wife who understood that on a night like tonight, a man might need to get out and enjoy a couple of beers with his friends; a healthy family;

a beautiful horse he'd practically stolen from Jamie Johnson, a guaranteed Grand Prix winner or his name wasn't Wyly King.

Never mind all that nonsense with Eddie and Grace. When he had dropped by Eddie's office earlier, just to chat, Eddie had told him that Grace was cooking his dinner tonight. Dinner? Just the two of them? He had winked at Eddie. Any fool could guess what *that* meant. Why, right now, they were probably tumblin' between the sheets, as happy as the day they had got married.

The song ended, and Wyly belched up beer. He turned into the driveway and noticed a van passing him from the opposite direction, with the word LOCKSMITH painted on the side. The driver gave him a friendly wave as he drove by. Wyly waved back and chuckled, wondering whether it was Emma Rae or Georgia who had locked herself out of the house.

He was tired now, eager to be in bed and asleep. He got out of the car and started toward his house. It took a moment for him to realize that Georgia had forgotten to leave a light on for him, as she usually did when he was out late. With only a sliver of moon, the steps were an obstacle course in the darkness. He swore softly as he stumbled on the top step and felt for the doorknob.

He pulled on the door and almost fell backward down the steps. The damn thing was stuck. He pulled again, but the door stayed shut. Not stuck, damnit! It was locked. He pounded on the door, rattled the knob, and yelled, "Mother! Something's wrong with this goddamn door!"

"There's nothing wrong with the door," came Georgia's response. "And don't call me 'Mother'!"

He could tell that she was standing just on the other side of the door, in the front hallway. "Then open the goddamn thing," he shouted.

"You go to hell!" she loudly declared.

"Georgia?" In all their thirty-eight years together, he had never heard her use a single cuss word. "What's goin' on? Open the door!"

"Why don't you go try Annie Pritchett's door?" she yelled.

He scratched his head and wondered whether the two bottles of beer had affected his hearing. Or maybe Georgia was the one who had had too much to drink. "What in the hell are you talking about?" he demanded. "Have you been into the apple wine?"

He heard the lock click, then the door swung open a couple of inches. He tried to push it further, but there was a new addition—a chain lock that was still firmly latched.

Georgia glared at him through the narrow open space. "I'm talking about your extracurricular activities!" she said. "I'm talking about your lying and cheating extracurricular—"

"Now, wait a minute!" he broke in. "I do not

cheat! I may have fooled around a little, but I have never cheated!"

"How could you do it, Wyly? Annie Pritchett was a friend of mine! I'm on the church auxiliary with that woman! And the girls! Grace and Emma Rae . . ." Her voice trailed off.

"Open the door, honey," he said gently.

She shook her head. "They think I'm a *fool!*" she said sorrowfully. "And I am! All the years . . . And there were times, Wyly, when I had thoughts, but never once, out of respect for you and our marriage . . . ! And now, I wish I had! I've been an utter fool!"

He could barely follow her, she was speaking in such strange, choppy fragments. "Now, don't say that! You're not a fool, honey . . ." He realized with a sudden flash of comprehension what she meant. *Thoughts?* "What thoughts?"

"Dr. Lewis. Frank Lewis. After all these years, he still has feelings for me! Especially since his wife died. He said . . . he said I have beautiful hips!"

Had to be the apple wine, though he didn't smell it on her breath. It was hard to take all this very seriously. What could have gotten into her tonight? He bet that looking at all those home movies had gotten her to realize she wasn't as young as she used to be. Hell, he didn't care. He was still just as crazy about her as the day they'd met.

He smiled to himself. "Honey, I wouldn't hang

any hopes on something somebody said forty years ago."

The smirk on his face was the last straw! "*Last week* he said it! When I took Aunt Rae in, I had my yearly physical. He said it last week!" she indignantly informed him.

His grin vanished instantly. "All right, that's enough!" he bellowed. "Open the goddamn door! I've been workin' like a hired hand all day!"

"The only thing you've been workin' all day is your big mouth!"

He threw himself against the door, which only made the chain pull more tautly. "You open up right now! I won't tolerate this kind of disrespect after the day I've had!" he yelled.

He made a second, equally unsuccessful charge on the door.

What was it Grace had said at lunch . . . was it only yesterday? Something about swallowing handfuls of bullshit . . . Much as Georgia disliked vulgarity, she had to admit that the phrase precisely expressed what she had been doing almost since the first day she had married Wyly. Well, things were about to change here at the King Farms, yes, indeed, they were!

"Don't you talk to me about disrespect! You don't even know the meaning of the word! You self-centered old goat!" she said.

"Self-centered?" he growled, rubbing his shoulder where he had hit it against the door. "Who the hell do you think you're talking to? Haven't I given you every goddamn thing you're ever wanted? You think you'd have had this kind of life with Frank Lewis?"

Georgia slammed the door shut and pulled off the chain. She threw the door open and blocked the entrance to keep him from coming inside. Years of smothered resentments welled up in her. Grace's out-burst had been excruciatingly painful, but there had been a lot of truth to her words. Now, Wyly was going to get a dose of that truth.

"The life I'd have had with Frank Lewis would have included respect! My own daughters are ashamed of me! But I'll tell you something. I'm ashamed of you! You are an embarrassment! Our Grace, her life is falling apart, and all you can tell her is it's bad for business! You're a disgrace! You drink too much! You laugh too loud at your own jokes, and I'm going to tell you something, Wyly! You fart in your sleep! But I've accepted every one of your faults without complaint because they're a part of you, and I loved you! I was proud to be your wife. But now I am not proud! So if you have to come into this house, then so be it. But you better know that if you step across this threshold, I'm going to call down to that barn and have those boys come up and throw you out on your ass!"

He stared at her, absolutely speechless.

She wouldn't have been the least bit interested, even if he had come up with a response. She stepped back into the house. The door slammed in his face. This time, it stayed shut.

～

For a second, Grace thought she was hallucinating the image of Wyly weaving in front of her car as she pulled into the driveway. Then she realized, yes, it really was her father, and she jammed on the brakes just as he grabbed hold of the hood to make her stop.

He ran around to the passenger door and tried to open it, but it was locked. He banged his hands against the window and motioned for her to roll it down. As soon as it was open a crack, he grabbed the top of the glass and began pulling on it, as if to make it go faster.

"They're crazy! All hell's broken loose!" he shouted.

He must be drunk, she decided, trying not to panic. "What happened? What are you talking about?"

"They're all holed up in there having a witches' coven!" He gestured wildly toward the house. "Your mother's gone completely off the deep end!"

Her mother! She thought, *Oh my God!* Whatever was happening, it was all her fault. "Daddy, let me go! Let me go up there!"

"She's way off the wall on this one! It's the goddamn squirreliest—"

"Dad!" she screamed. "I've got to go see her!"

He wouldn't take his hands off the window. His fingers were still gripping the edge as she pushed the button to roll it up.

"I am kicked out! Of my own goddamn house! You believe that?"

"Let go!" she screamed, and finally he did, just as the window reached the top of the frame.

He watched her speed off to the end of the driveway. "Oh, God," he mumbled. It was the damndest thing he had ever seen. "All the women have gone crazy."

Through the rear-view mirror, Grace watched him shaking his head and smacking tree trunks, as if they were somehow to blame. Ahead of her, the house stood dark and gloomy. She pulled around back and saw a dim light shining through the kitchen window.

She jumped out of the car, knocked at the back door, and was relieved to find Emma Rae there, along with Georgia, Aunt Rae, and Eula.

"You missed a really good time," said Emma Rae. "Although I hear you had quite a party yourself."

"The bug?" she asked, concerned about Caroline being left alone at Emma Rae's house.

Emma Rae pointed to the ceiling. "Upstairs."

Except that everyone was being unusually quiet, the scene didn't appear to be too out of the ordinary. Contrary to Wyly's dire ravings, Georgia seemed very tired but composed. Grace's heartbeat began to return to normal.

"Mother, please," she said, quickly crossing the room to join her at the table. "I'm . . ."

Georgia put her fingers to Grace's lips and shook her head: no apologies were necessary. Grace stared at her mother, marveling at her ability to forgive. Filled with love and wonderment, she pressed Georgia's fingers to her lips and kissed them. Tacitly, they communicated to each other the recognition that somehow, together, they'd weather even this crisis.

"Is he still roamin' around out in the yard?" asked Aunt Rae.

Grace nodded. "Yeah."

Eula set out cups and saucers for tea. "It's times like this that make you really appreciate being single," she said.

"Why doesn't he just go to a motel?" asked Georgia.

"It's a territorial thing, Mama," said Emma Rae. "He's probably out there pissin' on trees."

Georgia was about to scold her for using such coarse language, but abruptly changed her mind. Aunt Rae and Eula began to chuckle. Then Ema Rae started to giggle madly, which got Grace started. Soon, even Georgia was chortling, and then they really couldn't stop. They were slapping the table and holding their sides and gasping for air. And suddenly, nothing seemed quite so awful as it might have, because they had one another to laugh with.

The teapot whistled. This, too, would pass.

7

The Winter Grand Prix was a county-wide, three-day holiday. At King Farms, it felt more like a three-ring circus. Georgia ranked the weekend just below Christmas, Easter, and the Fourth of July in terms of importance. The attendees depended on her to observe certain customs and rituals. Just because she had kicked her husband out of the house, and her son-in-law was still nursing a bad stomach, she wasn't about to disappoint them.

The competition gave her a wonderful excuse to dress up and show off the farm. The barns shone with a fresh coat of paint, and colorful blossoms bloomed in every flower bed. Because their home was only six miles away from the Grand Prix show grounds, Georgia and Wyly always welcomed veteran participants to use it as an annex to the course. Even in Wyly's absence, the tradition still held, and by Thursday morning, the entire property had been temporarily transformed into one large parking lot for horse trailers.

The place was crawling with owners and trainers from all over the country. People were working their horses in the ring, in the driveway, in the fields—anywhere they could find enough space to trot, jump, or even walk them. Other visitors milled about, grabbing a few minutes to gossip, trade information, perhaps even negotiate a deal.

The actual meet events began tomorrow and ended on Saturday, with the prestigious Grand Prix championship, which was followed by Georgia and Wyly's annual bash. Before then, a dizzying amount of equipment had to be packed up and transported to the fairground. Hank took charge of the horses, while Dub and the rest of the grooms methodically loaded everything from canvas awnings and brass name plaques to furniture and clothes racks onto the Kings Farms trailers.

Grace's job was to make sure that the registration papers, rider numbers, and other documents didn't get lost in the shuffle. One year, long before she had become stable manager, the rider numbers had somehow disappeared from the barn. They had turned the place upside down, searching the office, stables—even the house—for the missing papers, but they were nowhere to be found. Wyly had raved and ranted about what he would do when he got his hands on the culprit responsible for misplacing the numbers, and they had all lost sleep over whether their entries would be disqualified by the officials.

They had turned up just in the nick of time, the night before the first event. Charlie Medans, who owned the roadhouse most often frequented by Wyly and his friends, had found them in a dark corner behind the bar, precisely where Wyly had stashed them for safekeeping.

Grace and Emma Rae could still laugh themselves silly recalling Wyly's sheepish expression after Georgia had given him Charlie's message. But the lesson had sunk in, and Grace made sure to personally deposit the all-important boxes of documents into Emma Rae's car.

It took her two trips, and then she was done. On her way back to her office, she waved at Jamie, who was loading his truck with his tack boxes. They had both been so busy that she hadn't seen much of him since the other night at Emma Rae's. She figured that by now he must have heard about Eddie and wondered how he felt about women who almost poisoned their husbands.

Eddie . . . She sighed. He was out of the hospital, and Caroline had reported that he was feeling better. But she hadn't heard from him directly, and she didn't dare call him. With all the work and excitement that preceded the Grand Prix, she had managed not to think too much about his parting words to her at the hospital. It was all too much to worry about right now.

She walked into the barn and caught Caroline at Possum's stall, cooing into his ear as usual and plying him with carrots. Georgia had mentioned that Caroline was still nursing her hope of riding Possum instead of Miss Lily. Exasperated, Grace lifted her off the mounting step and shooed her out of the stables. If Caroline had nothing better to do, she could go help her grandmother. One last thing, Grace added. She was *not* riding Possum, and that was final!

~

An hour later, the caravan of trucks, trailers, and cars pulled out of the driveway and rolled down the road. A pouting Caroline had announced that she was going with Grandma, which suited Grace just fine. She and Emma Rae were bound to get stuck in the massive traffic jam that always formed a couple of miles down, as everyone converged on the exhibitors' entrance to the show grounds. The last thing she needed was to be held a captive audience while Caroline pleaded her case for Possum.

Caroline's chattering at least would have been a distraction, she realized belatedly. Emma Rae was doing her best to keep the conversation light and funny. But suddenly, for no reason other than she was actually sitting still for the first time in days, she was hit with a devastating wave of sadness and longing for everything she and Eddie had so heedlessly discarded. She hadn't cried since the night at the hospital, but now she turned her head and stared out the window and wept for everything she had lost or never had.

~

The awnings were up in the show barns. The horses were fed and in their stalls, where the brass nameplates had been hung to identify them. All the equipment had been unloaded. The decorations committee, on which both Grace and Georgia served, had finished placing plants and flowers around the hospitality area. Grace had sorted out the paperwork and had set up a makeshift office in her locker in the changing rooms.

Almost everyone else who had finished setting up had left for town. Thursday night before the Grand Prix was traditionally party time. Even people who weren't remotely interested in horse jumping showed up at one or another of the bars to celebrate and unwind with the exhibitors.

Grace's plans for the evening involved nothing more ambitious than hitching a ride home and going to sleep. Exhausted and grateful for the quiet, she sprawled out in a chair to gather her energy. She had almost dozed off when Emma Rae charged into the changing room with a look on her face that meant she wouldn't take no for an answer.

"Come on," she said. "Get up. You're comin' with me."

~

The bar was crowded and smoky. As soon as she walked in, Grace knew she had made a mistake, but Emma Rae had given her no choice in the matter. She threaded her way through the throngs of people, until she finally found an empty table for two toward the back. While Emma Rae went off to buy them drinks, Grace waved at old friends who were in for the weekend and tried to look as if she weren't the most miserable woman in all of the South.

After a few minutes, when Emma Rae didn't reappear, Grace glanced around and noticed her sister deep in conversation with a tall, blond, good-looking man in jeans and Chiffowboy boots. Emma Rae was grinning, and the man, whose head was thrown back in laughter, seemed delighted to be talking to her. Reluctant to disturb her fun, Grace plastered a smile on her face and decided she would stay for another ten minutes, and not a second more.

She didn't last more than five before she turned back around and caught Emma Rae's eye. She pointed to her watch, signaling that she wanted to leave. Emma Rae, without tearing her gaze away from her new friend, held up a finger. "One minute," she mouthed.

Grace nodded okay, though it wasn't. The noise and hilarity were wearing away at whatever remnants of self-control she had left. She felt herself crumbling, her grief welling up inside, the tears about to flow again. She rubbed her eyes. It absolutely would not *do* to cry in front of everyone. She was about to get up and flee to the ladies' room when Jamie suddenly sat down next to her and leaned across the table.

"Okay," he said. "Just act like I just said something so funny you're about to die."

For no other reason than she felt as if she *were* about to die, she began to tremble all over. She glanced up and saw that Eddie was standing near the front door of the bar, surveying the scene. She laughed feebly at the absurdity of the situation, and then she started to cry.

Jamie leaned in closer to her. "I'll just sit here like I'm waiting to zing another one in there," he whispered.

Tears were streaming down her face. She hoped she was putting on a good show for Eddie, making it look as if she were laughing so hard, she was about to lose it. She wiped her face with a napkin, and suddenly, she was feeling so giddy that she really was laughing and crying at the same time.

When she looked over at the door again, Eddie was gone. Good, she thought. Let him think she was having the time of her life.

Emma Rae had elbowed her way over to them. "What's so funny?" she wanted to know.

Grace, who was still laughing uncontrollably, shook her head to say, *I can't talk*.

"I just have that effect on people," Jamie said, grinning.

Which really set off Grace, who flopped over the table and weakly beat the top with her fist.

Emma Rae stared uncertainly at her. "Hey, Grace," she said. She prodded her sister's shoulder to get her attention. "Do you think you could get a ride home, 'cause . . . uh . . ." She nodded her head in the direction of the guy she had been talking to.

Jamie's grin broadened. "I got it," he said.

"Oh, good." Emma Rae winked at him. "Thanks." To Grace's back, she said, "I'll see you tomorrow." Then she whispered to Jamie, "I wouldn't let her drink any more."

She motioned for her young man to follow her out of the bar. Grace raised her head as they passed by. "Have fun!" she giggled, and then she burst into tears.

Jamie waited a few seconds to see whether she could pull it together again. "Oh boy," he said, finally. "Well, I don't know about you, but I've had about all the fun I can stand. What do you say we head out of here? Okay?"

No response. His only clue to her condition was her hand, groping on the table for another napkin.

"Okay." He decided for them both. He stood up, helped her out of her chair, and steered her out of the bar and into the street.

The cool air helped clear her head. By the time they were in his truck and on their way back to the farm, she was feeling calmer—and more than a little embarrassed by her fit of hysteria. She rested her face against the window frame and felt the wind ruffling her hair. Bonnie Raitt was singing about love and loss. She thought, *Tell me about it, honey.*

"Is this a tape?" she asked, studying Jamie's profile.

He turned and smiled at her. "Yeah."

He had a nice smile. Not the kind of *too* nice smile that she would be afraid to trust, but warm . . . friendly . . . inviting.

They reached the turnoff for the farm. He drove down the road and stopped in front of Emma Rae's house. He leaned back against the seat and turned to face her. She thought about hugging him again and shivered.

"Is this where you wanted to go?" he asked.

"No," she said softly.

"Oh. Well. Where do you want to go?"

"I don't know." She rubbed her finger over her wedding band. "I don't feel like going home yet."

"Well," he said hesitantly. "I'd invite you back to my place for a nightcap if—"

"Okay," she said.

"Okay." He smiled at her and nodded.

She smiled back and decided that maybe tonight she would find out what it felt like to kiss him.

He was staying in the empty tenant house, which was little more than a small, one-room cabin at the edge of the woods, at the far end of the road that curved behind her parents' house. The door creaked as they stepped inside. When he turned on the light, she saw that the place was clean and tidy, except for the shirt on the floor, which Jamie immediately grabbed and rolled into a ball.

"Wow. It's been a long time since I've been in here," she said.

"Wasn't expecting company," he said, self-consciously sticking the shirt behind his back.

She grabbed it out of his hand, threw it back on the floor, and grinned. She circled the room, touching the few pieces of furniture, all of which were the same as she recalled them. "God. Everything seems smaller."

"Yeah, it's kind of close quarters in here," he said. "You want a drink?"

He sounded nervous, which struck her as funny, because she felt so comfortable being there. She nodded yes to the drink and said, "I used to play in here when I was little. And then later . . ." She smiled to herself, remembering how she had played there when she got older.

"I think there's some glasses here somewhere."

He opened and closed cupboards in the tiny kitchen until he found some.

"I lost something in here," she said, gazing wistfully at the pull-out bed.

"Yeah?" He poured two bourbons and handed her a glass. "What was that?"

"My virginity," she said and clinked her glass to his. She drained the whole glass in one shot and handed it back to him.

He stood motionless, staring at her as she wandered over to the window next to the bed, conjuring up the memories.

"God, I was fifteen . . . fourteen . . . no, fifteen, because that was the year I rode Miracle Child in the National. He was here with his parents to buy a couple of studs. Everybody was off at the auction."

He cleared his throat. "Uh, would you like another drink?"

She nodded, and he handed her his untouched glass. "I remember I was so nervous," she said, slowly sipping the bourbon. "I was standing right here in this very spot, with my back to him, looking out the window. I knew I wanted something to happen, but I didn't know what to do or say. So I just stood here, hoping and waiting for him to make his move."

He came up behind her, and she felt his arms come around her waist.

"And?" he said, so softly she almost didn't hear him.

She closed her eyes and leaned back against his chest and relaxed into his embrace. The warmth of the bourbon was working its magic. She felt loose and happy for the first time in days.

"And finally, he did," she murmured and turned to face him. She threw her arms around his neck and kissed him, long and passionately, as she had been wanting to do since that night on Emma Rae's porch. Emboldened by the bourbon, she pushed him onto the bed, but her aim was poor, and he hit his head on the wall.

"Sorry," she mumbled between kisses, but he didn't seem to mind, because he was kissing her back with an ardor that matched her own.

Still locked in his arms, she started undoing his buttons. But as she got further down his shirt, her mind got the better of her lust, and her courage began to fail her. Furious with herself, she lay still, with her hand hovering just at the point where his shirt met his pants.

"What's wrong?" he whispered.

"Nothing," she assured him. *Everything.* She popped open the last button and was immediately seized by a fierce spasm of guilt.

"Fuck you, Eddie!" she shrieked. She leaped off the bed. "Fuck you!"

Startled by her outburst, he bolted upright and glanced around, expecting to see her husband.

They were alone in the cabin, but Eddie was there with them in spirit. She felt him—or was it her conscience?—jabbing a finger at her, accusing her of adultery and disloyalty. "I have absolutely nothing to feel guilty about! I was not the one who was unfaithful! Right?" she demanded of Jamie. "Am I right?"

"Right," he said, stretching his arm out to her.

She sat down next to him, pulled off his shirt, and started unbuttoning her blouse. "I mean, I *want* to do this!" she said, trying to convince herself. "I really want to!"

He wanted to believe her. "Good."

He covered her face with feather-soft kisses as he gently helped her with her buttons. She liked what he was doing and wanted more of it. Ten years with the same man . . . more, if she counted the year and a half they'd been together before they got married . . . she'd forgotten how other men felt, smelled, tasted.

He slipped off her blouse, drew his fingers across her camisole, and stared at her. Excited by his touch and his gaze, she lay down. But the second her head touched the pillow, she felt Eddie's presence again and had to sit up to set matters straight.

"But you know," she said, speaking as if he were right there in front of them, "it just figures that the one time I would want to do this, you'd figure out a way to take the fun out of it! I am *not* doing this for revenge!" She pointed at Jamie. "You are not a revenge fuck! Let's get that straight right now!"

"Okay."

"That is *not* what's going on here!" she declared emphatically.

He wasn't so sure. "What *is* going on here?"

She started to answer him, then swiftly shut her mouth. What a good question he had asked. If only she had as good an answer. She shook her head. "I have absolutely no idea . . ."

"Come here." He patted the bed and put his arm around her when she rejoined him.

"I mean, this is crazy," she said, leaning against his shoulder. "I've been wanting this."

He sighed. He hated what he was about to tell her, but it would never work. "Well, I can't believe I'm about to say this, but you aren't ready."

"Oh, yes, I am," she said, wishing it were true.

"Oh, no, you're not," he said resignedly. "Listen, I know about this. You're going to have to face facts. You've got a broken heart. You have to deal with it. And I don't want to be this crazy thing you did one night."

She wasn't sure whether she felt worse for him or for herself. "Are you sure?"

"Grace, you're so damn beautiful, it pains me," he said, shrugging on his shirt.

"Shit." She could have kissed him again just for

saying so. Instead, she asked, "Well, then what do you want to do?"

"I don't know. What do you want to do?"

It was still early. So much adrenalin was pumping through her veins that she could have run a marathon. She might not be destined to make love with him this evening, but she was having too much fun to call it a night. She was starving. She had eaten very little for lunch, even less for dinner. She knew exactly what she wanted to do next.

~

"Oh, God," Jamie moaned. "You were right. This is better than sex." He took another bite of Eula's pecan pie and chewed it slowly, relishing every morsel as judiciously as a wine connoisseur might savor a fine vintage wine.

Grace set two glasses of milk on the table and held a warning finger to her lips. Her mother and Caroline were asleep upstairs, and she didn't want either one of them coming down to disturb her party. "God, save me some!" she giggled as Jamie helped himself to more pie directly from the baking dish.

"It's a *whole* pie!" he said.

"So?" She dug her fork into the pie. "I want to tell you something. If you can't eat half this pie, then you're a damn Yankee."

"I can eat half. At least. Just keep your toes and

fingers out of the way." He chuckled and began to make good on his boast.

"Shh . . ." She grinned, enjoying the play of shadows on his face cast by the dim light from the corner table lamp. She hadn't had this much fun since college, when she and Emma Rae would make late-night raids on the refrigerator and compare notes after their dates. "Thank you, Eula," she whispered.

"Thank you, Eula." He nodded his agreement. "I'll say one thing, you Southern women sure are easy to please."

"I guess that's what comes from centuries of being bred to keep your expectations low." She laughed, then did a wicked imitation of one of Wyly's favorite maxims. "'Honey, you gotta learn to recognize your limitations.'"

He smiled dryly. "Well, you know what they say: 'Recognize your limitations, and sure enough, they're yours.'"

That was a new one for her. Her laughter died with a suddenness that surprised them both as she absorbed the full impact of its message.

"Oh, shit," she said and stared at him with the wild-eyed gaze of someone who had just discovered the world was round, and she wouldn't fall off the edge if she kept on sailing. "Holy shit!"

She ran to the hallway and charged up the stairs as if she were being pursued by a pack of rabid dogs.

Her daughter lay fast asleep in the narrow twin bed of Grace's own childhood. A beam of light shone across the covers as she quietly slipped into the room and shook her gently awake.

"Caroline, wake up," she said in a low, urgent whisper. "I have to tell you something."

Caroline burrowed further under the covers, resisting her mother's voice. Grace shook her again, more insistently, until her eyes flickered open. Dazed with sleep, she stared slack-mouthed at Grace and struggled to pull herself upright.

"You're going to ride Possum," Grace told her. "Okay?"

Caroline nodded unequivocally, threw back the covers, and stood up.

"Not right now, sweetie. Tomorrow," she said, helping her back into bed.

"Do you know I love you, bug?" she whispered.

"Yes," Caroline said sleepily.

"All right, baby. Good night."

"'Night," Caroline echoed.

Grace kissed her and tiptoed out of the room. She stopped a second in the doorway to stare at Caroline, who was scrunched up under the covers, hugging her pillow. Then she closed the door and started back downstairs. She was halfway there when a loud, high-pitched squeal from Caroline's room sent her rushing back up the stairs.

The light was on in the room. Caroline stood in the middle of the bed, both arms raised in an exultant V, poised for the victory that was already hers.

~

Georgia's special touch was evident in the gracious atmosphere of the King Grand Prix show barn. The area around the entrance was carefully landscaped with daisies, hyacinths, and tulips. Just inside and to the left was a comfortable sitting area for family members and visitors, with leather chairs and a full bar. But on Friday afternoon, no one was taking much advantage of the amenities.

Grace and Emma Rae, all dressed up as was Grand Prix custom in their best hats and suits, were too busy fussing over Caroline, as they and Hank completed their inspection of her gleaming leather boots and brand-new riding habit. Grace was almost bursting with pride and love for her daughter, who stood calm and composed, in sharp contrast to the three adults, with their frazzled nerves.

"Now, he has a tendency to back off at the first fence," Emma Rae reminded her, "so keep him in front of your leg—"

"—and trot him all the way to the end and let him see the course." Grace threw in her own quick piece of last-minute instruction.

Caroline smiled as serenely as if the first-prize medal were already hanging around her neck.

"Hi, Daddy!" she called out, spotting Eddie as he walked into the barn.

"Hey, doodlebug!" Eddie gave her a big hug and managed to greet his wife with barely a glance in her direction. "Grace."

The moment felt as awkward for her as it seemed to be for him. "Hey, Ed." She nodded, glad to see that he looked well, with no obvious side effects from the food poisoning.

Trying to ease the stiffness of their meeting, Emma Rae reminded Caroline. "From three to four is a bending line. It's set on the half stride and . . ."

As she droned on about details that Caroline had long since committed to memory, Eddie motioned Grace to move a few steps away from the others. "You should have discussed this with me before you let her do this," he said quietly. "I'm her father."

Stung by his implied criticism of her judgment, she snapped, "I know who you are, Eddie."

He looked directly at her for the first time since he had walked into the barn. His icy cold gaze, reflecting the depths of his fury, frightened her. "Oh, no, you don't."

In the background, she could hear Emma Rae, still playing the instructor to a bored Caroline. "I think you should get the five, so keep him on the outside track."

If they had still been together, she could have

made the decision for Caroline to ride Possum, and Eddie never would have said boo. She was surprised he even realized that Caroline had switched horses—or that he cared.

"Look, I'm sorry," she said, hoping to achieve a truce. "It happened kind of suddenly."

"I don't care. Don't let this happen again," he said curtly, and walked back to Caroline.

She followed him numbly, stunned by his brusqueness.

"You'll feel him going into it," Emma Rae was saying. "So just support him at the vertical—"

"Okay, ladybug," Eddie broke in. "I'm going to go watch. Go in there and—"

Emma Rae threw him a dirty look, as if to say, *What could you possibly tell her about being in the ring?*

"—have fun." Eddie finished his sentence. He wrapped his arms around Caroline and gave her a big hug and a kiss.

She glanced from him to Grace. "Hey, kiss each other for luck," she urged them. "I mean for me."

Grace felt rooted to the spot, too mortified to move. Caroline stared expectantly at them until, finally, Eddie came over and gave her a perfunctory kiss on the cheek. Then he waved at Caroline. "I'll see you out there," he said, and strode out of the barn.

Grace's cheeks were flushed with anger and embarrassment, but she was determined not to

178

spoil this moment for her daughter. She kissed the top of her head and straightened her collar. "Now, just focus and listen to Hank, and you'll be—"

"Please, just go watch," Caroline said. "Okay? Just let me do this. I want to do it by myself."

Grace and Emma Rae looked at Hank, who nodded. He understood their message: they were trusting him with Caroline's life.

Grace leaned down and hugged her. "You come from a long line of winners, honey," she whispered. "Me and your Aunt Em, we used to run this joint."

Caroline shook her off and pulled away. "Just watch."

179

8

~

The horses from the previous class were just clearing the ring when Wyly showed up at the family's railside box and took a seat at the back, behind the rest of his family. His arrival was met with smiles from his daughters and Aunt Rae, but Georgia ostentatiously peered through her binoculars and refused to acknowledge his presence.

"All right, ladies and gentlemen." The announcer's voice boomed over the loudspeaker. "Coming into the ring is our next class, number 93, the 2500-dollar Winter National Youth Jumper Classic!"

Grace exchanged a quick glance with her mother. Caroline had competed before in plenty of meets, but never one of such importance or degree of difficulty. Nor had she ever competed on a horse whose personality was as hot as Possum's. For the first time, she understood what Georgia had gone through all those years when she and Emma Rae

180

were blithely jumping their way to the winners' circle, never once worrying about broken bones or cracked skulls. She sent up a quick prayer that she had made the right decision and clenched her fists.

"Don't forget to breathe," Georgia murmured, patting her hand.

Grace nodded gratefully and turned to scan the crowd for Eddie. She found him about two-thirds of the way around the ring and tried to make eye contact. She may as well have been invisible, because he gave no sign of seeing her as he smiled and greeted friends who stopped to say hello.

The way he was treating her, she was lucky he hadn't pressed charges. She shuddered, recalling his suggestion that she hire a lawyer. He'd meant a *divorce* lawyer, she reassured herself. He was furious with her, but she couldn't imagine that he would want to see her in jail.

She sneaked another look at him, wondering whether he had brought a date. She almost wouldn't put it past him. But though he was surrounded by people, he didn't seem to be talking to anyone in particular, and her very worst fear wasn't realized: there was no trace of Miss Red Crepe Suit.

~

Along with the other riders entered in the Youth Jumper Classic, Caroline waited impatiently in the warm-up ring for her number to be called next. By far the youngest and smallest in the group, she sat self-confidently astride Possum while Hank held his bridle and did one final check of the tack. Possum's tail flowed smoothly, and his mane was neatly braided, according to Grand Prix regulations, which took notice of such details in the judging of each entrant. He rechecked her stirrups and patted Possum on the neck. There was nothing more he could do now, except send Caroline into the ring with his blessings.

A round of applause signaled that the previous contestant had finished her jumps. "It's about that time," Hank said.

Caroline nodded. She was ready.

The announcer was calling for number 105, Caroline Bichon on Silver Bells. Hank led her toward the course and gave her a pat on the leg. Then he stood back and watched her trot into the ring.

Caroline took a second to gaze around the packed arena, then silently told Possum to give it all he had. They were a team. She trusted him totally to stay calm and not get spooked by the brightly colored rails or oddly shaped standards. She had no doubt but that they were going to win this one together. She bent forward from her hips, moved her hands up the reins, and told him to fly.

Grace almost did forget to breathe as she watched her daughter's face, a study in pure concentration. Caroline was a blur of motion, gliding easily over one jump after another: verticals, oxers, walls, and aichens. Grace glanced quickly at Eddie, hoping to share this experience with him. But once again, he kept his eyes fixed on Caroline and refused to meet her gaze.

"That's it, that's it, don't override him," Hank whispered, his eyes, too, riveted on his young student.

Grace and Emma Rae's lips were also moving with silent instructions. But Caroline didn't need any of them to guide her through the course. She had planned this day with Possum for as long as she could remember, and she had listened intently to everything Hank had ever taught her. She knew exactly how to adjust herself to Possum's stride, so she was right there with him as he increased his power before each jump.

They lined up for the last series. Grace held Emma Rae's hand as Caroline sailed cleanly over every one of them. A second later, she was up and out of her seat, screaming along with the rest of the crowd, cheering her daughter for what had to be the best moment of her life.

"And that's a clean round for number 105," declared the announcer. Caroline flashed an ear-to-ear grin and patted Possum's sweaty back.

"There you go, honey," Georgia said as the audience continued to roar its approval. "There's your accomplishment."

Grace shook her head. "Mom, that's not my accomplishment. It's hers."

"No, baby, *she*'s your accomplishment. She's as worthwhile as anything you've done with your life."

Her gaze still riveted on Caroline, Grace nodded agreeably, more to be polite than because she believed a word of what her mother was saying. She wanted to believe her. She wished she could accept that she was even the tiniest bit responsible for Caroline's fearlessness and faith in herself. But she had made such a muddle of her life. She had rejected so many choices because it was easier and safer not to take any risks. The possibility that she had a positive influence on her daughter seemed much more grounded in fantasy than fact.

~

"Announcing the awards for the 1995 Winter National twenty-five-hundred-dollar Youth Jumper Classic. Carrying on that family tradition, first place goes to number 105, that's 105, Caroline Bichon riding Silver Bells!"

The audience was applauding again as Caroline rode Possum around the ring to the winners' circle. Hank was already there, waiting for her, as were the officials who were going to present her award of a silver tray.

"I told you I was ready," she reminded Hank.

184

"Oh, I knew it," he said proudly, smiling up at her. "All along."

Her family and rest of the crowd watched as the first prize blue ribbon was pinned to Possum's bridle, and the winner's sash was hung around his neck. Caroline held the silver tray aloft.

"That's my granddaughter!" Wyly boasted to anyone in the stands who would listen.

The announcer declared, "Let's hear it one more time for our youth riders and our champion, Caroline Bichon, on Silver Bells as they take their victory gallop!"

As the audience yelled and cheered, Caroline rode out into the ring again, followed by the other prizewinners, and cantered around the perimeter of the course. Approaching her family's box, she slowed to a trot and touched the brim of her hat, just as she had seen Wyly do in Georgia's home movies. As if they had rehearsed the move, the family stood up en masse and rewarded her with their own special prize, the salute that recognized she was carrying the winner's tradition into the next generation.

~

Caroline was so excited she couldn't stop talking for a second as she and the rest of her family headed back to the show barn. She had to tell Hank the whole story, every detail of every jump, and after him, her mother and Emma Rae and her grandparents.

Wyly was more interested in making peace with Georgia. He caught up with her and Aunt Rae, and artfully tried to drape his arm around her shoulder. But Georgia had her stubborn side, too, and she wasn't ready to forgive and forget. She dipped away and slipped out from under him, leaving him to scratch his head and wonder what it was going to take to make her see reason.

"Caroline! Come here for a minute!" called Grace.

Caroline stopped in midsentence and danced over to give her mother another hug.

"Mama gave me this first time I won in my fourteen-and-under class," Grace said, pinning a tiny gold horse to Caroline's riding coat.

Caroline touched her finger to the horse's miniature tail. "Are you proud of me?"

Grace was taken aback that she needed to ask. "Of course, baby. I was proud of you before."

"Gramps said I got the talent!" Caroline whooped.

"You most definitely do!" Grace agreed.

"You know how it is when you just know you're supposed to do something, and if you don't do it you just know you can't feel happy?"

Grace smiled to hear so much simple wisdom coming from such a little girl. "Yes," she said. "I do know."

Caroline suddenly caught sight of Eddie, who was standing just outside the barn. "Daddy!!" she shouted and went running to meet him.

Grace watched Eddie scoop her up and spin her around in his arms. She trailed them into the show barn, thinking that the three of them were supposed to be celebrating as a family. Eddie and herself together enjoying Caroline's triumph and sharing her joy. Instead, they were separated by a deep trough of antagonism and nastiness. Was this now how it would always be between them, until they got so old that neither could remember what had caused the breach in the first place?

She banished such bleak forebodings from her mind, if only for the evening, and surveyed the party which was just starting to swing into gear. Georgia was greeting well-wishers and pointing to the bar, where Wyly had already helped himself to a drink. He had commandeered Caroline and was showing her off as if she were his protégé, regaling their visitors with tales of her glory. Emma Rae was pouring champagne for Georgia and Aunt Rae.

"Just a little drop, now," said Aunt Rae. Emma Rae complied as always with their ritual. "More . . . a little more . . ." urged Aunt Rae. "Just a skoshe more . . . keep going."

Emma Rae kept going until the glass was full to the brim. "That's good," said Aunt Rae, delicately bringing it to her mouth without spilling a drop.

Wyly stopped bragging to his guests long enough

to walk across the room and offer Eddie his congratulations in the form of a hard slap on the back. He handed his son-in-law a drink, but Eddie shook his head no thanks.

Grace saw their interaction and winced. Eddie wasn't one to turn down a drink on such an occasion—unless his stomach was still sore from all that vomiting. This was ridiculous, she decided. He was her *husband*, goddamnit, not some stranger whom she was forbidden to approach. She could at least apologize, take the first step in mending the rift. Even if they didn't stay married, they had to stay friends, if only on account of their daughter.

"Pretty good, huh?" she said, coming to stand next to him.

He smiled, watching Caroline launch into yet another retelling of her win. "Yeah, it was. Incredible." He turned to face her and said, "Grace . . ."

She held her breath.

"I want her to come home tonight," he said.

The idea didn't compute. "Tonight?"

"You've had her all weekend."

"But she's going to want to come to the show tomorrow night," she said, grasping for any good reason to say no.

He glared at her. "I know that! But she wants to come. I don't want to fight about this."

But tonight, of all nights? She had been so looking forward to tucking Caroline into bed and

188

spending time alone with her, talking about how well she had ridden, how impressed she had been by her handling of Possum, how much she admired her courage. She had imagined them giggling together until Caroline fell asleep.

Now Eddie wanted to deprive her of these small pleasures . . . except that he had said that Caroline wanted to go with him. But surely she hadn't come up with the idea herself! And why did he have to sound so damn cold and matter-of-fact, as if she were some business associate of his?

She forced herself to stay calm. "No, I don't want to fight either. I think it's probably a good idea," she lied. "I'm just a little . . . surprised, that's all."

"Yeah, well, sorry about that, but it came up kind of suddenly." He quoted back to her what she'd told him earlier about her decision to let Caroline ride Possum.

She felt as if he had punched her in the face. "Eddie, why are you talking to me like this?" she asked, fighting back tears.

Just at that moment, Caroline glanced over and saw them huddled head-to-head. She smiled broadly and waved at them. Grace waved back, and so did Eddie, both of them smiling as if they were having a marvelous time together.

"All right, look," said Eddie. "Monday morning, we'll get our lawyers to work out a visitation schedule. Then there won't be any more surprises."

There was a limit to how much she could take of his insulting tone and words. If that was how he wanted it, then so did she. "Fine, Eddie. Call June and have her schedule it," she said, the coldness in her voice matching his own.

Intent on getting the last word, she wheeled around and went to join her mother, Aunt Rae, and Emma Rae, knowing he wouldn't dare follow her over there. She had barely recovered her composure when Mrs. Pinkerton scurried over, her camera slung around her neck, her elbow hooked around Wyly's arm.

"I'm so glad you're all still here!" she chirped. "Let me get a picture of you all together!"

Her innocent request was met with a strained silence. *All together* was not exactly their strong suit, just at the moment. But their reluctance went completely unnoticed by Mrs. Pinkerton, who was motioning for Eddie to come over.

"Hank, you get in there, too," she said as the trainer tried slinked past.

He ignored her and kept on walking. But for Caroline's sake the others grouped themselves into a cozy configuration, with their young star standing smack in the middle.

Mrs. Pinkerton took her time adjusting the lens and fiddling with the light meter. "Smile," she said finally, just as the smiles were starting to crack.

For the one second it took to flash the picture, Eddie put his arm around Grace.

"Y'all have such a wonderful family," Mrs. Pinkerton gushed.

Georgia, Eddie, Emma Rae . . . Each of them shot off in a different direction, as if propelled by hot gasses.

Only Grace didn't move. She stood alone on the spot where seconds earlier all the people she loved most had enacted their faked tableau of a happy united front. She had never felt so utterly helpless. She and Eddie had turned each other into enemies, and there didn't seem to be anything she could say to make it better between them. Thanks to her big mouth, Georgia wouldn't even deign to look at Wyly, and she couldn't do anything about that, either.

But there was one situation over which she still had some control, she decided, and went looking for Hank. She found him in the changing room, emptying out his locker.

"Hank, I have to talk to you," she said.

He didn't even bother to look up.

She had had enough of being ignored for one evening. She pushed him into a tack room, closed the door, and told him exactly what was on her mind.

~

A wan-looking Aunt Rae lay propped up against a pile of pillows, sound asleep in one of Georgia's guest rooms. Frank Lewis stepped away from the bed, removed his stethoscope, and wordlessly indicated to Georgia that his most persistent patient was going to be just fine.

Georgia sighed with relief. Frank had warned Aunt Rae time and again about drinking too much champagne. The bubbles went right to her head, and then she got so giddy she couldn't keep her balance. It wasn't a heart attack or a stroke he was worried about, but rather that one day she would fall flat on her face and break a leg or hip, and then she would really have him at her beck and call.

She was just a little tipsy and tired, too, from all the excitement of Caroline's victory. He made her sip a glass of baking soda and water, along with a couple of aspirins, and promised he would be by in the morning to see her. The words were hardly out of his mouth before she was gently snoring.

Georgia smiled her thanks at Frank. Even in the dim lit from the bedside lamp, she didn't fail to notice how handsome he was. He was tall and lanky, thinner than Wyly, and very distinguished with his thatch of silver hair. As she led him out of the room, she smoothed her hands over her hips and hoped that he was admiring the view from behind.

For a few seconds, their shadows were visible through the window, long enough for Wyly, drunkenly pacing the front yard, to catch a glimpse of them. He lurched forward and shook his fist and howled at the moon for revenge.

He was unaware that he had an audience. Grace and Emma Rae sat in the darkened living room on either side of the sofa that faced the window, watching their father's performance. Inspired by his jealousy, he was talking to himself, shadow-boxing, and bumping into trees and shrubs.

"He is the silliest son of a bitch on two legs, isn't he?" said Emma Rae.

"That's a roger," Grace agreed.

They lowered their voices as Georgia and Frank Lewis came into the hallway. They could hear their mother thanking him, and then the front door creaked open. They saw Wyly stumble toward the porch, where Georgia and Frank stood quietly talking.

Wyly strained to eavesdrop on their conversation, but all he caught was the sound of Georgia chuckling softly in response to something Frank had said. It had been a long time since she had chuckled so enthusiastically at any of *his* jokes, he thought resentfully. He trotted up to the door, hoping he might insinuate himself into their discussion, perhaps even slip past Georgia and finally get back into his own home.

Georgia was too swift for him. She knew all his old tricks, and she wasn't about to let him inside on a night when he reeked of bourbon. She said a quick good night to Frank, slammed the door in Wyly's face, and threw the lock.

Thwarted by his own wife, Wyly hiccuped his protest and concentrated on Frank Lewis. "Well, Doc, is she okay?" he asked.

The doctor nodded. "Oh, yeah. You get to be that age, and you get a little excitement, have a little too much punch, but she's okay. She'll outlive us all."

"Well, that's good. That's fine," said Wyly, slightly slurring his words.

Frank Lewis waited for him to say something else. But Wyly just swayed gently from side to side and kept quiet.

"Well, call me if you need to. And good luck tomorrow night," said the doctor.

"Hey, Doc?" said Wyly as Frank Lewis stepped past him to leave. "Did you say she had beautiful hips?"

The doctor looked slightly chagrined. "Well, yes I did," he admitted. "I meant for . . . well, she does. And you know, I delivered both your girls so I've seen—"

Wyly had heard enough. Frank Lewis had no cause to be telling him what he'd seen of Georgia's anatomy. The man was a menace. Had to be silenced. Only one way to do it. He swung hard, but there was no contest. The doctor was sober and more sure on his feet than Frank had been in hours. He nimbly stepped out of the way. Wyly toppled over and sprawled flat on his face.

Georgia, who had been monitoring the scene with her daughters, cried, "Oh, my Lord!"

"Stay here, Mama!" said Grace.

She and Emma Rae raced outside. By now, Wyly had managed to pull himself back up and was trying to throw a right hook at his rival.

"It's all right!" the doctor yelled. He struck a pose with his fists clenched in front of his face. "I boxed in the navy!"

Grace grabbed Wyly and, without too much effort, pinned his arms behind his back. "Daddy, stop it! Jesus Christ!"

Aunt Rae, perfectly healthy and alert, was positioned at the upstairs window. She craned her neck to catch the action, until the sound of footsteps on the stairs sent her scrampering back into bed. When Georgia peeked in to check on her, she had resumed her prostrate position and pretense of sleep. Not even Dr. Lewis could have guessed that she had staged the whole show, fainting spell and all, just to get Wyly's goat and put a little color in Georgia's cheeks.

She would have been gratified to know how well she had succeeded. He was still blowing hard as Frank Lewis pulled out of the driveway. Weaving unsteadily, he tried to ease himself down next to his daughters on the porch. But he missed his footing, tipped sideways, and landed with a hard thump that didn't do much for his sciatica.

"That son of a bitch better not come around here 'less he wants to get his ass kicked," he grumbled tipsily. "That no good son of a bitch!"

Grace and Emma Rae exchanged knowing looks. It wasn't the first time they had had to haul him off to bed, and it probably wouldn't be the last. They stood up, one on either side of him, and pulled him to his feet.

"C'mon, Daddy. There's more ass to kick tomorrow. You can rack out at my house tonight," Emma Rae said.

Wyly flopped his arms around their shoulders and allowed himself to be led toward the carriage house. "Can't even sleep in my own goddamn bed," he mumbled.

"Daddy, I talked to Hank tonight," said Grace.

"Good." Wyly gave a resounding burp. "You get him all squared away?"

"Yeah."

"He's not gonna quit?"

"No."

"Good," he grunted.

He didn't ask why, but she told him anyway. "Because he's riding Ransom."

He stopped so short that she almost fell herself.

"What?" He reeled sideways, trying to face her. "Now why would you go and say a fool thing like that? You think you can make that decision without even discussing it with me?"

"There's nothing to discuss," she said flatly.

His anger cleared away the effects of the alcohol. "I'll do exactly with my own goddamn horses as I goddamn please!" he said, sounding stone cold sober now.

Maybe down the line, but not this time. Today and tomorrow, at least, she was still the stable manager. Her mind was made up. "I'm not doing your dirty work anymore, Daddy. Hank rides."

"Why do you think I've been doin' this for all these years? My health? All I've ever wanted is to just once, win that. Don't you have a loyal bone in your body?" Wyly shouted.

She had thought it through, anticipated all his objections. She knew him so well. "Loyal to a fault," she told him. "You want to win? Great. But if you want the respect of me or anybody else in this family, you're going to have to win it fair and square."

"So now you've got it figured that the stable manager tells the owner what to do?" He shook his head incredulously.

"No. I quit. I'm going back to finish vet school. I'm telling you as your daughter. As me."

She inhaled deeply. The air smelled so sweet. Lord, how she loved this place. But it was way past time for her to leave.

Whatever else happened, she had to quit waiting

for someone to come along and rescue her from Rapunzel's tower. She couldn't remember how the fairy tale ended. Did Rapunzel let down her golden hair and climb into the arms of a handsome prince? Or did she take a chance and fly free, trusting that in all those years she had watched the world go by, she had gathered enough strength to find her own path through the woods?

It was so quiet that she thought she could hear the gurgling of the creek that ran way behind the stables. She used to love following that creek until it disappeared underground at the eastern boundary of their property. She wondered whether Caroline had ever explored the creek, whether the water still ran as cold and clear.

"You want me to drag the sorry son of a bitch the rest of the way?" asked Emma Rae.

"No! I'd rather crawl," Wyly declared, sighing hugely.

"Come on, Grace." She grabbed her sister's hand and led her back to the main house. "Now, doesn't that feel good?"

"It really does," Grace said.

"You girls," Wyly mumbled. "I swear to God."

He never would have guessed Grace had the guts. Or maybe he would have. A girl who showed so much spunk on horseback had to be plucky enough to stand up for what really mattered. She had inherited that from him, just like her sister.

He smiled and went off to the carriage house to

get some sleep. He had a big day ahead of him. He was about to beat the hell out of Hank Corrigan on a beautiful scopey horse who was going to carry him straight to the winners' circle.

9
~

The gate to the show ring swung open. The field of competitors surged onto the course. Riders and trainers walked in pairs, studying the terrain, familiarizing themselves with the jumps, planning their race. Grace walked with Hank, not because she had much advice to offer him, but because she didn't want him out there alone, with no show of support from anyone at King Farms.

The judges based their decisions first and foremost on form and technique. But they were only human, and particularly in cases where two entrants were scored very closely, the tiniest element could make the difference between first place and reserve.

Grace twice passed Wyly and Jamie as they came around the circle. The first time, she was concentrating so hard they were only a vague presence at the periphery of her vision. But the second time around, she glanced up and caught what she imagined to be a wink of approval from Jamie. She wasn't sure for what: Eula's pecan pie? her show of strength for Hank? Or maybe he was just saying a friendly "hi," and wishing her luck, so long as it wasn't better than his.

She felt surprisingly calm, considering all that she had been through the day before. She hadn't seen Caroline yet today, but Eddie had promised to bring her to the box, where Georgia, Aunt Rae, and Emma Rae had probably long since taken their seats.

The red-coated ringmaster approached the viewing stand to confer with the meet officials. Grace noticed him pointing to his watch. The moment had come to clear the ring and close the gate. The Grand Prix was about to get under way.

It was standing room only in the arena. The atmosphere was taut with anticipation. Georgia especially was having a nervous fit, behaving so peculiarly that Aunt Rae kept wondering aloud whether she ought to summon Frank Lewis to bring his smelling salts.

"Well, here we are, ladies and gentlemen." The announcer called the crowd to attention. "Here's what we've all been waiting for."

The audience roared its agreement.

"Yes, it is," the announcer reiterated. "So let's welcome the Winter National Grand Prix competitors into the ring!"

Hank was set to ride sixth. Standing backstage,

where the riders were practicing their jumps and milling nervously about, Grace tracked each entrant's progress on the course according to the reaction of the crowd. Applause meant the rider had completed a clean jump; a noisy gasp signaled a missed jump or a bad spill.

Standing next to Hank, she could feel his tension as if there were an electrical current running between them. There was no reason to be so anxious. She had seen him on Ransom hundreds of times. He knew the horse, knew his likes and dislikes and quirks. Whether or not Harvey was a better jumper was beside the point. Wyly hadn't yet spent enough hours with him.

"You've got it in the bag," she said and gave him a quick hug.

Wyly cracked his knuckles, put his foot in the stirrup, hopped up onto Ransom. They were ready to rock 'n' roll.

". . . and now horse number 1434, King's Ransom of King Farms, Wyly King, owner, trainer Hank Corrigan in the irons," roared the announcer.

The crowd gave an ear-splitting cheer for their longtime favorite as Hank rode out into the ring. The women in the King box applauded wildly. Caroline hooted and stuck two fingers in her mouth to try to whistle. Even Eddie got caught up in the drama.

The arena grew quiet as Hank lined up for his

first jump. He cleared it beautifully. Across the ring, Grace caught Caroline's attention. Caroline held up her hands to show she had her fingers crossed for luck. Grace nodded and suddenly discovered something new about being a parent. There could come a point when the relationship might shift, as it had now, for her and Caroline. For this moment, they weren't simply (as if it ever could be simple!) mother and daughter, but also two people consumed by the beauty and competitiveness of the sport.

She saw something else, as well. Eddie was watching the exchange between her and Caroline. But when she started to smile at him, he glanced back at Hank, who proceeded to make another clean jump.

He was into the final series now—a brick wall with matching standards; an aichen; and a panel painted with a bright blue-green abstract design. Grace thought, hey, whatever it takes, and crossed her fingers behind her back.

He gave a flawless performance. A thunderous cheer went up when he finished. "That was a clean round for King's Ransom! Number 1434," the announcer declared. "We'll see you in the jump-off!"

The excitement was almost palpable in the King box. Caroline was bouncing up and down, unable to contain her glee. She gestured to Grace that she wanted to come stand with her by the gate. Grace nodded and signaled, "Come on!"

"Daddy, I want to go with Mom," said Caroline, starting to climb over the seats.

Eddie looked at Grace, who motioned for him to send Caroline over. He shook his head no. He wanted Caroline to stay right where she was, and not go running around in the middle of all these people.

Grace was annoyed that he was making a fuss over something that was so silly, yet mattered so much to Caroline. And to her, too, she realized. She wanted Caroline there by her side, to experience all of this with her. She gestured for him to look at Caroline, who was pleading for permission to leave the box.

Finally, he agreed, but Grace could tell even from the distance between them that he wasn't happy about it. She wondered why he cared. He couldn't talk horses with Caroline. He had never bothered to learn the language. He barely knew how to ride, though she had often offered to go out with him so he could become more comfortable in the saddle. Were they now going to spend the next ten years ripping at each other and having power struggles over Caroline?

Caroline also felt his displeasure and worried that she might have hurt his feelings by not wanting to stay with him. "Daddy, can I ride with you to the party?" she asked, trying to make it up to him.

"Yeah. We'll see," he said absentmindedly.

Georgia put on her bifocals and studied the program. "Well, there's three more till Wyly. I'm going to the little girls' room," she said. "I'll walk you halfway, Caroline."

"I'll see you later, bug. You stay with your mother," said Eddie as Caroline and Georgia exited the box.

Emma Rae leaned back and tapped him on the knee. "You know, Eddie, I just had a flash."

"I'll alert the media," he said sourly.

"I'll bet that one day, you and Grace will make fantastic grown-ups. You want a Coke? I'm going to get a Coke."

He shook his head and watched her go, not knowing what to make of her comment.

"Are you bringing Caroline to the party?" asked Aunt Rae.

"I'm pretty sure Grace doesn't want me there, Aunt Rae," he said.

"Oh." She sniffed. "Suddenly you're an expert on what Grace wants."

"No, I'm an expert on what she doesn't want." He stared moodily across the ring and saw that Caroline had found Grace, and that they were talking to Hank. He felt left out, though of what, he didn't know. It hadn't occurred to him to come to the party, but maybe he would reconsider.

Georgia threw one hell of a party. He would sure hate to miss out on a good time, all because he wasn't on speaking terms with his future ex-wife.

~

"Just stay loose. Ride it one fence at a time," Jamie said as he checked Harvey's bridle and straightened his noseband.

Wyly adjusted his helmet and watched Jamie fussing with the tack. "I know," he said.

The boy needed to relax. He himself felt wonderful. Never better. He had slept like a log and awakened feeling as fit as a man half his age. That first prize trophy belonged to him. They may as well engrave his name on it right now, so he could stick it over the fireplace right after the race. That was another thing that was going to get settled tonight. He missed his bed. He missed Georgia. He wanted to go home.

"I know you know," said Jamie. "But I'm saying it anyway!"

He held Harvey's reins while Wyly mounted him and wished he were the one riding Harvey today. "All right. Let's go do it."

Grace hurried over while her father waited just outside the ring for his number to be called. She patted Harvey on his shoulder and glanced up at Wyly, who was grinning with excitement. He gave her a slight nod, enough to tell her they were fine.

This was too good a moment for him to be holding a grudge.

The announcer beckoned him into the ring. "And finally, number 1365, Have a Heart, King Farms, James Johnson, trainer, and owner Wyly King up!"

The crowd greeted him with a clamorous round of applause. One look at him, so handsome and regal astride the magnificent horse and Georgia's heart skipped a beat. "Oh my God . . ." she breathed.

Aunt Rae overheard her exclamation and patted her arm. "It's just a man on a horse, baby girl, nothing more," she said. "Just a man on a horse."

For Aunt Rae, maybe. But Wyly was still her white knight, riding out to slay the dragons. His armor might be slightly tarnished by now, but he was the same dashing young man who had courted and claimed her. She loved him, plain and simple. Her heart was with him every second, and she whispered encouragement to him as he galloped around the course.

All eyes were on Wyly. He was riding with supreme self-confidence, adjusting himself to Harvey's aggressive stride.

"Let him come forward," Jamie muttered, chewing his nails.

The tension was building in the arena. Grace and Jamie traded glances. She knew what he was going through. Her father had accused her of being disloyal, and perhaps she was, because part of her wanted more than anything for Hank to win. But she also wished that Wyly could achieve the goal that had eluded him for so many years.

He took the last group of jumps, flying over each one as if Harvey had sprouted wings. The audience gave him a resounding burst of applause. Georgia let out an audible sigh of relief that drew a disdainful look from a disgusted Aunt Rae.

Even the announcer seemed momentarily to have lost his neutrality. "And there it is, ladies and gentlemen. Another clean ride for King Farms! Wyly King, number 1365, on Have a Heart! And have a heart he does!" he declared.

Grace and Emma Rae caught each other cheering for their father and shared a grin. In spite of everything that had happened, they couldn't stop themselves. He could drive them nuts. He could irritate them beyond all endurance. But first and foremost, they were—and always would be—Wyly's girls.

~

Georgia's eyes were closed in prayer. "Dear Lord, please let the right thing happen," she whispered. She had resisted the temptation to go down to the backstage waiting area during the intermission and pay Wyly a visit before the second round. She was sorry now. He might have been expecting her, and she wouldn't want to have jinxed his next ride. But she could still pray for him, and leave it up to the Lord to decide what the outcome should be.

The rider currently in the ring was trotting back toward the gate. She had completed a clean round, and the crowd applauded its approval. Wyly had barely said a word to Jamie the whole time the woman had been in the ring. Grace, watching him from across the waiting area, decided she had never in her life seen him stay so quiet for so long.

Now it was Hank's turn to show whether he could maintain the excellence of his previous round. Grace held Ransom's bridle as he mounted the horse. "You're a good boy," she murmured to Ransom. "Give him the ride of his life."

If Hank felt any jitters, he didn't show it. He looked very strong as he headed toward the gate, and he stayed strong, moving toward the first vertical jump.

Grace lingered at the gate, vicariously jumping every obstacle with Hank, silently urging Ransom to keep calm. She knew the horse could do it. She felt his eager energy as if she were the one sitting on his back. Ransom was a born competitor who thrilled to do battle in the glare of the spotlight. He had been trained to give his all. She understood his hunger to win. She had had that hunger once herself.

While Jamie spoke quietly to Harvey, Wyly stood by himself, listening for the crowd's response.

Hank was the man to beat. There was no question in his mind about that. The other entrants were window-dressing. This was a Grand Prix people would be talking about for years to come. He felt absolutely sure of himself, almost cocky enough to call out to Georgia from the ring, "Watch me win this one, honey."

He didn't need to remind her. He knew she was watching. He could feel her rooting for him.

The arena rang with applause, signaling the end of Hank's round. From the sounds of it, Wyly guessed his timing was good, as well.

He sprung up into the saddle and waited for Hank to clear the ring.

"Good luck, Daddy," said Grace, coming into the staging area as he was heading out.

Wyly smiled. "No luck to it now, darlin'. Now, it's all skill."

He was still smiling as he passed Hank going through the gate. "Good ride, son," he said. He could afford to be generous. Hank was a good man and an excellent trainer. It wouldn't hurt the farm's reputation one bit to have him come in second to Wyly's first place in a national Grand Prix.

He rode out onto the course and took a moment to fully drink in the thrill of the moment. He surveyed the audience, picked out his family's box, and found Georgia, waving madly at him. Caroline sat next to her, and he was sure he could see her grinning. She should be grinning. The Kings were going to own the '95 Winter Grand Prix.

He pressed his thighs against Harvey's flanks and headed for first place.

His family may as well have been riding right alongside him. They didn't take their eyes off him for a second as he lined up for each new obstacle, caught quick glimpses of the time clock flashing by, sailed neatly over the different shaped and colored jumps.

He was doing well, but not well enough by his reckoning to beat Hank's time. The final series, the triple rails, still lay ahead. He could easily make the time up there by giving Harvey a little extra push.

He approached the rails at a center and inclined his body forward. His hands were light on the reins, his torso almost parallel to Harvey's back. He could feel Harvey judging the distance, lengthening his stride to carry them over the jump.

He took off with his legs tucked well under him. He had almost cleared the rails when he faltered for the scantest quarter of a second. Wyly felt the hesitation at the same instant that Harvey's left back hoof flicked against the rail, just hard enough to send it spinning to the ground.

The crowd groaned in sympathy. Georgia bent down to pick up her purse and hide the tears that sprang to her eyes on her husband's behalf. An enormous grin spread across Hank's face as he stood up and silently thanked the Lord for giving him his win.

"And that makes four disappointing faults for number 1365, Have a Heart," declared the announcer as Wyly retreated from the ring. "But still a win for King Farms with number 1434, King's Ransom becoming this year's Winter National Grand Prix Champion!"

The arena went dark, except for the spotlights that played across the ring. The audience bellowed its approval.

"And let's welcome him into the winners' circle. Hank Corrigan and King's Ransom—the new one-hundred-thousand-dollar Winter National Champion . . ."

As Hank and Ransom rode into the winners' circle, the entire arena rose to give him a standing ovation.

In the confusion of all the noise and darkness, Grace searched the staging area for her father. She was glad, for Hank's sake, that he had won first prize. But she grieved for Wyly, knowing how pained he must feel. This was supposed to be Ransom's year, and the victory was well deserved. Wyly had tempted fate, and lost. But even that was a lesson worth learning. At least he had tried.

Another year, it might be his turn to stand in the glare of the spotlight, exulting in the acclaim of the crowd. She knew he would be back for another shot at the chance to be hailed as the champion.

Someone was calling her name. She was wanted in the ring. She hurried outside to accept congratulations and a trophy on behalf of King Farms. She managed to give Hank a quick hug before he was whisked off to be photographed with Ransom in all their victory finery: a white sash around Ransom's shoulders; a medal for Hank; a blue, red, and yellow first-place ribbon on Ransom's bridle.

There was still no sign of Wyly as the announcer proclaimed the second-place winner. "Reserve Winter National Grand Prix Champion is 1925, Sharper Image! Owned by Sheila and Martin Adrian, and Brian Scott, and trainer Sherry Mack in the irons!"

Georgia clutched Emma Rae's hand. Wyly must be devastated. To lose to Hank was one thing, but to come in third . . . She started out of the box. She had to find him.

"Third prize goes to 1365, Have a Heart, King Farms, Wyly King owner and up, trainer James Johnson," the announcer said.

And there he was, because like it or not, he had to take his turn in the circle to accept his third-place yellow ribbon. He managed a wan smile, then stood to the side while Hank posed for more photographs.

"Ladies and gentlemen," the announcer boomed. "Our 1994 American Winter Grand Prix

Champion—King Farms, number 1434! King's Ransom! Owner Wyly King, ridden to victory by trainer Hank Corrigan!"

Sporting a wide grin, Hank led the victory gallop around the ring, accompanied by the screams and applause of the entire arena. People surged forward to congratulate Georgia and the others. Georgia smiled and nodded her head, but all she wanted to do was get Wyly and bring him home. The victory ride had to be the final indignity, having to trail behind in third place while Hank got the lion's share of recognition.

Of course, she could have told him that entering Harvey was a mistake. But he hadn't consulted her, and he would only have shooed her away if she had offered her unsolicited opinion. Stubborn Wyly. He would never learn. But so what? She had married him for better or for worse, and she would still take him over any man in the country—and that included Frank Lewis.

~

The revelry was in full swing at the show barn. Hordes of people were stopping by to celebrate with the Kings and toast their double victory. Champagne corks were flying in every direction, and the drinks were freely flowing. Wyly arrived, all smiles, to shake Hank's hand and mumble something about having to go change.

As Grace came in with Caroline in tow, Dub

and the other grooms were toasting Hank and Ransom. Caroline threw herself into Hank's arms and hugged him so hard that Grace almost had to pry her off his neck. When she did at last let go, it was Grace's turn to be enveloped by Hank in a bear hug that only ended when someone started pouring another round of champagne.

Georgia was busy making sure that everyone was well taken care of. She had caught only a brief glimpse of Wyly when he had first come in, and she kept peering around the room, trying to locate him in the crowd. Finally, she called over Emma Rae, asked her to make sure everyone had enough to drink, and went in search of Wyly.

He hadn't gone far, only next door to the changing room. He had just removed his hat and was dusting it off when she opened the door. He was turned away from her, but she saw that his shoulders were heaving. She came up behind him and rested her head on his beck. She heard the sobs he was trying so hard to muffle and wished she had the power to banish his pain.

As if he had read her mind, he turned and embraced her. "It's not about the horses," he mumbled.

She loved him even more for telling her. "Come on, honey. Come home," she said in her most soothing voice.

~

The party in the show barn was only the warm-up act for the main event back at the farm. An enormous tent had taken over the entire lawn behind the main house, which was ablaze with light. Georgia had designed the flow of traffic so that people came in through the front foyer, where dozens of candles cast a beautiful, warm glow, and walked through the house to the backyard.

More candles flickered on the tables that were scattered through the tent, which had been divided into a dining area and a dance space. Many of the guests were already dancing to the live band, while others were lined up at the two long buffet tables, which were heaped with barbecued beef, country ham and redeye gravy, Eula's homemade biscuits, corn on the cob, mashed potatoes, and collard greens. Between the two tables stood a slightly smaller round one, in the center of which was Georgia's declaration of independence, an enormous pile of shrimp flown in fresh that morning from the Gulf.

Drink in hand, Wyly circulated through the crowd, bellowing greetings and entertaining everyone who crossed his path with tales of Hank's riding genius and Ransom's greatness. The music already had people jumping and sweating. Caroline and her friends were doing a line dance that had them in fits of giggles, until, at Emma Rae's request, the band began to play "I Could Have Danced All Night," a song that was popular the year her parents got engaged. Like a magnet drawn to steel, Wyly found Georgia among the crush of people and led her onto the dance floor. She fit her head into the crook of his neck and followed his lead, as if they had been dancing together all their lives, which they just about had.

Grace studied them from the edge of the floor and thought how much in love they still looked after almost forty years. She wanted that for herself, too. She glanced around the tent. Eddie was nowhere to be seen.

Emma Rae stopped to say hello to Aunt Rae and her friends, who were clustered at one of the tables, making sure that Georgia's shrimp didn't go to waste. She left laughing at one of Aunt Rae's jokes and came over with a glass of champagne for Grace.

"Well done, sweetie," she said.

"Thanks." Grace sipped the champagne. "Is that guy coming?"

Emma Rae shook her head. "You think I'll ever find a guy that underneath it all isn't secretly hoping I'm helpless?"

Grace smiled and kissed her sister's cheek. No one deserved a fabulously wonderful man more than she did. "It's inevitable," she assured her.

Their parents waltzed by and blew kisses. Behind Wyly's back, Georgia winked at them.

"That's the thing you got to love about Daddy," said Emma Rae. "Even when he loses, he wins."

She raised her glass and clinked it against Grace's. "To vet school."

Grace drank to that, and to whatever else her future might hold.

~

It figured that Jamie would be sulking in the barn, since that's exactly where Wyly would have gone to hide at his age, in his situation. He was slumped on the floor of Harvey's stall, his elbows on his knees, looking like he needed to get drunk or laid. Or maybe both.

Wyly leaned over the door of the stall. "Son, I guess you're right. I don't know my ass from Bakersfield. Or is it shit from shinola?"

Jamie shrugged. "Either way," he said, making it clear that he wasn't in a company mood.

He was just a kid. He had a lot to learn about the important things in life. He'd kind of hoped that Emma Rae and Jamie might get interested in each other, but evidently there were no sparks between them. But if he didn't have a woman, at least he'd have a horse.

"You take him back with you," Wyly said. "Next year, take him in there yourself. I'll pay you your rate. When you're ready, I'll sell you half of him." He chuckled at Jamie's stunned expression. "I only do 'bout one decent thing a year, so I suggest you take me up on it. Now, come on up to the house and have a drink, son. You've earned at least that."

His business finished, he wanted to get back to the party. But Jamie made no move to follow him. He didn't like mopers. Shit happened to people. You had to get over it and move on.

"Come on. Let this horse get some rest," he ordered him.

Jamie got up and shook his hand. He was grinning as he hurried along to the party with Wyly.

The place was really hopping now. Jamie went looking for Grace and found her talking to some woman who didn't look as if she had even so much as sat on a horse.

"Hey." He tapped her on the arm. "Dance later?"

"Check." She smiled, looking forward to it.

He went over to the bar and bumped into Hank. "Congratulations," he said, shaking his hand.

"Thanks. Really." He clapped Jamie on the back, trying to let him know he understood his disappointment better than almost anybody.

"I'll be glad when this goddamn year is over," Jamie said.

Hank nodded sympathetically. "Next year, man."

~

Eddie still wasn't sure whether he belonged at the party, but since he was there, he was going to have a few laughs if it killed him. What he hadn't counted on was Wyly wanting to have a heart-to-heart talk with him. He knew he was in for it when his father-in-law bore down on him and clamped his hand on his shoulder.

"Son. You know, sometimes a man doesn't know the value of what he's got till he's lost it. Do you follow what I'm getting at?" Wyly asked.

"Hey, Pot! Kettle! Pleased to meet you." The guy had nerve. You had to admire him for that.

Now that he had patched things up with Georgia, Wyly was determined to make Eddie do the same with Grace. "I'm not sure you fully understand your responsibilities," he said gravely.

"Really?" Eddie asked sarcastically. "What do you think I'm doin' here? That I came here to have fun?"

Wyly nodded, though he hadn't a clue about what Eddie was getting at. He tried again to make him see what he had only just learned himself. "Well, things are gonna be changing around here. You understand what I'm saying?"

"Amen, brother," Eddie intoned.

Their talk hadn't gone exactly as Wyly had planned it. Puzzled by Eddie's response, he went to ask his wife for another dance.

"And congratulations on getting to sleep inside!" Eddie called after him.

On the other side of the tent, Grace spotted Eddie conferring with her father and wondered what they were up to now. She was surprised that Eddie had showed up and hoped that he didn't have any more nasty surprises in store for her. She forced herself to focus on Mary Jane, who had been stuck for an interminably long time on some issue about the cookbook.

"So what's the question? It's between the sweet potato pecan pie or the strawberry chiffon?"

"No, we want to use them both. It's just . . ." Mary Jane chewed her lip. "How do you want your name listed?"

Her manner made Grace suspect she had something else on her mind besides recipes. "Why are you asking me this?"

"Well, the cutoff for the printer is Monday afternoon . . ." Her voice trailed off. She looked around, as if hoping somebody would come by and hand her a drink.

"And?" Grace prompted her.

"Well, Grace, not to put too fine a point on it," Mary Jane said boldly, "I heard you and Eddie were getting divorce."

Grace almost dropped her champagne glass. "How did you hear that?" she demanded.

Pleased to be a source of information for Grace, Mary Jane stepped closer and lowered her voice. "Well, Edna told Nadine who told Kitty who told me that she'd seen Eddie having lunch with Jack Pierce, who is the meanest son of a bitch divorce guy in town, and you should try to hire him if Eddie hasn't, because when Betsy and Beau

Barkley split, he screwed her to the wall. I mean, she got squat!"

Grace was so mad she could have spit. But Mary Jane was just the bubbleheaded messenger who was probably still stewing over Grace's revelations about Calhoun and his cocktail waitress. The true villain was standing across the room, yukking it up with one of his buddies.

"Mary Jane? I'm going to have to get back to you on the name thing," she said, as sweetly as she could manage.

"You know the really weird part?" Mary Jane's tone positively dripped sugar. "I always thought you and Eddie were the perfect couple. But if you ever need to talk . . ."

Grace didn't bother staying for the end of the sentence.

"Hi, Frank, how are you?" She gave his friend a perfunctory greeting, then said, "Excuse me, Eddie, I need to have a word with you for a second."

Before he had a chance to open his mouth, she pulled him into a far corner of the tent. "Eddie!" she whispered. "Mary Jane Reed just informed me that you and I are getting a divorce."

He shrugged his shoulders. "So what, is she psychic?"

"She said that you were seen having lunch with Jack fucking Mad Dog Pierce."

"Grace!" he said, loudly enough that she

shushed him. He lowered his voice. "I said we should talk to lawyers. You've talked to one, haven't you?"

"I've made an appointment to talk to one," she lied. "But that's not the point. Couldn't you just be a little more discreet?"

"Discreet!" he sputtered. "You ought to be fined five hundred dollars just for sayin' the goddamn word!"

Lord, she would never live that down! She hated for him to have something over her. "Okay, okay!" she conceded. "I just can't stand the idea of it being all over the damned barbecue. It's probably in the goddamn newspaper—"

"You're right! C'mon. Let's go put a stop to this right now!" he declared. He grabbed her wrist and pulled her toward the front of the dance floor.

"Eddie, what are you doing? Let go!" she whispered furiously, trying to break his hold on her wrist.

"No! Let's deal with this. Come on!" he insisted.

The band finished playing a slow, romantic ballad. In the lull that followed, the band leader said, "Okay, let's liven things up a little around here!"

"No, Eddie! No!" Grace said vehemently. After how they had once felt for each other, she couldn't bear to dance with him now that he hated her so much.

But it was too late. The band swung into a Motown tune, and Eddie had her trapped. He grabbed her hand and effortlessly twirled her around, in spite of all her efforts to resist him. He flashed her a devilish grin as he reeled her back in. She remembered that grin and knew just what he had planned.

"No! Don't you dare double dutch! Don't you dare double dutch, Eddie!" she yelled.

Her screams of protest only goaded him on to more mischief. He grabbed both her hands and, in perfect rhythm to the throbbing soul song beat, forced her to twist herself under the bridge they'd made of their outstretched arms.

He didn't know a thing about riding, but he was a world-class dancer. Even with her trying to get away from him, they were easily the best dancers on the floor. She spun in and out, up and over, in a dizzying succession of moves that sent her whirling back in time to their college days.

People were staring at them, she realized, as he flung out and away from him. And what a sight they must be, the soon-to-be ex-spouses cutting up like a couple of teenagers.

"I'm gonna kill you!" she yelled as he reeled her in.

"No, you're not." He grinned. "Okay, now sweep and 'round the world."

Everyone else had cleared the dance floor and formed a giant circle, with them at its center, spinning out of control like a couple of whirling dervishes.

"This is *not* funny!" she hissed as he pulled her toward him, grabbed her hand, and broke into a lindy trot.

"Yes it is!" he whispered.

And suddenly, she realized he was right. It *was* funny, and she was having a ball. She stopped fighting him and let her heart take over and her body follow. They were really moving now, dancing in perfect synch, the way they used to, the chemistry between them the same as it was in her photo album.

The song was almost over. "Up and over?" he asked.

"Roger," she gasped.

As if they had been practicing for days, he turned away from her and deftly flipped her up and over his back, landing with a deep double dip, just as the song ended.

There was a burst of applause, calls for an encore.

They stood inches away, staring at each other. They didn't need words to know that they were both feeling the poignancy of this intimate public hello and good-bye. If things had been different, they would have bridged the narrow divide between them with a kiss. But as it was, a kiss was out of the question.

The music started up again, a slow tune that brought people back onto the floor.

"A fitting end," she said sadly, thinking of the pictures from the frat party.

"I really am sorry," he said softly.

The spell was broken by Caroline, who threw herself in between them and grabbed Eddie by the waist.

"Dance with me!" she pleaded. "Dance with me!"

Eddie tore his gaze away from Grace and smiled at his daughter. Then he swept her up in his arms and glided across the room. Grace stared after them, panting for breath, feeling that now-familiar knot in her throat. They were her family. Without them, she was only one-third of a whole. She still wanted that wholeness. Didn't he?

An arm snaked round her shoulder. Surprised, she glanced up, and Wyly took her other hand and waltzed her onto the floor.

"Bet you didn't know you still had it in you!" he teased.

"Hey, Daddy," she said, full of emotions too deep to express.

"Hey, darlin'."

They danced silently for a minute as she pulled herself back together. Wyly held her against his chest in a tight, comforting hug. For once, he intuited what she was feeling.

"You looked good in there tonight," she said.

It was still a sore subject for him. "I looked all right."

"I was proud of you."

"Good," he said. "I was proud of you, too."

"Dad, I'm sorry." It wasn't exactly what she wanted to say, but that was as close as she could come right now.

"Don't be." He smiled.

She smiled, and the threat of tears lifted. "I'm not."

Eddie and Caroline were dancing a few feet away. He was spinning her around in a much tamer version of the steps he had danced with Grace. She threw back her head and laughed with such abandon that Grace almost couldn't bear to think of her ever growing up. Just then, a very pretty young woman in a tightly fitting sheath tapped Caroline on the shoulder, wanting to cut in. Eddie looked at her and smiled. Then he shook his head no, picked Caroline up, and whirled her across the floor.

~

It was getting late. The crowd had thinned out. Only the hard-core drinkers and dancers were left. The band was still playing, mostly slow songs. *Make-out songs,* Grace remembered they used to call them in high school. She had finally dragged Caroline off to bed in one of the guest rooms, and now Grace noticed Eddie leaving the tent, probably to go kiss her good night. She was about to leave herself when Jamie walked over to claim his turn on the floor.

"I can't dance like your husband," he warned her.

"Thank God." She laughed, oddly pleased that he had seen them.

They fell into an easy rhythm together that surprised both of them. He was a good dancer, though very different from Eddie. He was less demanding, less of a performer, and it made her wonder what he'd be like as a lover. When she lay her head on his chest, she could hear his heart beat. She closed her eyes, tucked herself under his chin, and followed his lead.

Her eyes were still shut as she glided past Eddie, who had been watching her the whole time she had been dancing with Jamie. His face was a mask. But Wyly, coming up behind him, could guess from his stance that his son-in-law was not a happy man.

"Well, son, you were lucky to get her the first time," he said cheerfully.

Eddie shook his head and turned away. "It was a damn miracle."

10

~

For old times' sake, because both of them were feeling very silly, Grace and Emma Rae had decided to sleep in their former bedroom. Surrounded by their childhood artifacts—the flowered wallpaper that was covered with horse photos and paintings and all their dozens of prize ribbons, they stayed up gossiping until they couldn't keep their eyes open. Grace instantly fell into a deep sleep and dreamed of riding Harvey bareback behind Eddie, her hair swirling loosely around her like Lady Godiva's.

Then the dream changed, and she was alone in a ramshackle old house, anxiously searching the rooms for Caroline, who was missing. She was frightened, not only because she couldn't find Caroline, but also because the house felt dangerous, full of howling ghosts and demons. The doors flapped open and shut, and when she climbed the stairs, the boards creaked under her feet. She stopped walking and closed her eyes, but the creaking continued, and she was sure someone else was in the house, following her, trying to stop her from getting to Caroline.

A door squeaked open. She forced herself to open her eyes, and suddenly she realized that this was no dream. It was the floorboards in the hallway she had heard creaking. There really was someone in the room, a man standing in the doorway, a few feet away from her bed. She opened her mouth to scream, and the man leaped at her and covered her mouth with his hand.

"Grace, it's me," Eddie whispered urgently. "For God's sake, please don't wake up Emma Rae!"

He put his finger to his lips to shush her and waited for her eyes to tell him that she understood what he was saying. Only then did he take his hand away. He crouched beside her on the floor.

"What are you doing here?" she whispered.

"I got to talk to you, Grace. I had fun tonight."

"Me, too," she said, wondering whether she was dreaming again.

"Grace, was there ever a time . . . ?" He broke off as Emma Rae turned over in bed. He flattened himself against the floor and didn't sit back up until he was sure that Emma Rae was fully asleep.

"God, just looking at her makes my nuts hurt," he murmured.

Their faces were so close, they were almost touching.

"What?" She wanted him to finish asking his question.

"Remember how crazy, how like, every night we used to . . . remember?" he whispered.

"Yeah."

"Okay. Remember the night you said we made Caroline? Remember you said you knew? That night? That you could feel that?"

"Yeah."

"I felt it, too. I wanted to tell you that."

"Okay," she said, feeling his breath on her face.

"And you know how I said . . . that when I asked you to marry me, I didn't think you'd say yes?"

Her heart hurt her every time she thought about that. "Yeah."

"I hoped that you would," he whispered.

"I did," she reminded him in a quiet murmur.

"I know. Don't you wonder if we could ever get back to that?"

She searched his eyes in the darkness, remembered how it once had been. She wanted to believe that he was telling the truth now, but she was as scared as she had been a few minutes ago in her dream.

"Yeah," she whispered. "I don't know."

"I don't either. But it's something to think about." He hesitated a moment. Then he said, "I'm gonna go."

"Okay," she said, feeling the lump of unshed tears in her throat.

He took her face in his hands and kissed her with such passion that the knot instantly dissolved. Their kiss was so deep that she felt as if she were falling down a long, dark tunnel, and he was all she had to hold on to.

"But try to remember," he whispered.

"Okay."

"I love you, Grace," he said. He sneaked out of the room as quietly as he had come in.

Her heart pounding, she listened to his footsteps in the hallway and stared at the dark empty space where he'd just been.

"Grace!" Emma Rae whispered from the other bed.

"I know," she said. She threw back the covers and tiptoed after him. "Eddie! Wait!" she called to him quietly. She tiptoed down the stairs, knowing exactly where to walk so as to miss the creaky floorboards. He waited for her at the bottom of the steps.

"Eddie? I remember everything," she said, pressing him against the wall.

"You do?" He sounded surprised.

"Every goddamn minute."

"John and Sue Coon's pool?"

She pressed her lips against his and tasted him. "Like it was yesterday. Tallu's place at Jekyll Island?"

He kissed her back, finding her tongue. "Oh, yeah," he moaned.

She wrapped her legs around him, and he picked her up and carried her into the living room. He brought her over to the sofa and lay down with her. She rolled on top of him and kissed him greedily, over and over again.

"Remember this?" he breathed.

She laughed and moaned with passion. "Tucker's field behind the grade school," he whispered.

She pulled away from him and said, "Where?" But when she saw the look of panic on his face, she took pity and laughed to show she was kidding, and he pulled her back down to kiss her again.

"Hilltop House at Harper's Ferry," she murmured as their bodies melted together.

"Right here, Grace," he said. "Right now."

They spent the night together there. They made love, as if for the first time, as if they had been saving themselves all their lives for each other and this moment. They were very quiet, so as not to wake anyone, but their eyes and mouths and bodies eloquently expressed their stifled cries of passion.

With whispered words of love, they rediscovered what they had always known, yet had somehow forgotten. There was a space in their hearts they had each carved out for the other, a place that could be filled by no one else. They talked and made love and laughed and made love again, remembering what they had shared when their love was still fresh and pure. They spoke of what they had become together, and how to mend what had gone awry. They avoided talk of the future, both knowing that their pain was still too raw to make plans or promises that might prove too difficult to honor.

He left at dawn, as the sun was just beginning to rise and the first hints of red and purple were showing on the horizon. She walked him to the door and breathed in deep mouthfuls of the cool morning air. Then she kissed him good-bye and hurried upstairs to her room. She slipped silently into bed, smiling and hugging herself as she listened to his car pull out of the driveway.

"Grace?" whispered Emma Rae.

"Yeah?"

"I remember," she said. "You had it bad."

~

One thing they could always seem to depend on was that no matter how fine and clear the weather was during Grand Prix weekends, the days following would inevitably be chilly and damp. It was Grace's personal belief that the gray, overcast skies were nature's way of expressing the letdown everyone experienced after so much turbulent emotion and high drama.

The dank, gloomy atmosphere contrasted sharply with her own hopeful, buoyant mood. She felt as if she were just embarking on a wonderful adventure, at once thrilling and unnerving, full of unpredictable twists and turns. She had no idea where her journey might lead her, and the unknowing only added to her sense of excitement.

Her first stop was the stables, where she went not to work but to collect Caroline for the jaunt into the woods she had been promising herself and her daughter for months. They decided to ride bareback—as she had done in her Lady Godiva dream, she remembered as they trotted out of the barn.

The yard was mostly empty now, the trailers packed up and gone. The farm felt oddly deserted, though most of the men were around and busy with various cleanup jobs. At the far end of the barn, Dub and one of the other grooms were loading Harvey into Jamie's trailer, which was already hooked up to his truck. Grace looked around for Jamie and saw him chatting with Hank. His duffel bag lay at his feet, and he appeared ready to leave. She rode over and hopped off the horse while Caroline took a few turns around the field.

"I'll bet you're glad to be rollin' out of here," she said, walking him to his truck.

"It's been . . . interesting," he said.

They smiled at each other, and then she said, "I'm glad we got to dance."

She heard the crunch of gravel behind her. Eddie's car was coming up the road. Though he had to have seen her, he didn't make the turn at the barn, but just kept going up the driveway toward her parents' house.

"I'll see you next year," Jamie said.

She nodded. "I'll be here."

He toed the ground with his boot. He didn't seem to want to leave. "Jump in," he said, pointing to the front door. "It's unlocked."

She smiled. Today she had other places to be. They hugged good-bye, and she thought about how good she had felt dancing with him.

"Maybe in another life, huh?" he said.

"You never know." She smiled. "This life's not over yet."

He gave her a funny, crooked grin and climbed into the cab of his truck. He turned the key, waved good-bye, and rolled out of the driveway. She watched the trailer until it disappeared down the road. Caroline came trotting over. She scooted forward, and Grace climbed onto the horse and took the reins.

They rode through the field toward the main house, where Eddie was standing in the driveway, as if waiting for them. He looked very serious, almost scared, until she smiled. Then he did, too, and the place she had made for him in her heart felt very full and warm.

She said, "I remember you."

There's an epidemic with 27 million victims. And no visible symptoms.

It's an epidemic of people who can't read.

Believe it or not, 27 million Americans are functionally illiterate, about one adult in five.

The solution to this problem is you... when you join the fight against illiteracy. So call the Coalition for Literacy at toll-free **1-800-228-8813** and volunteer.

Volunteer Against Illiteracy. The only degree you need is a degree of caring.